CHINATOWN CHRISTMAS

Chen Family Cuisine #1

KAILIN GOW

Kailin Gow

Chinatown Christmas (Chen Family Cuisine #1)
Published by Golden Scroll Entertainment; an Imprint of
Sparklesoup.com
Copyright © 2022 Kailin Gow

For information, please contact:
Sparklesoup.com

Get a Free Romance and notices of new releases from
Kailin here:

https://dl.bookfunnel.com/qgu4l0rizc
First Edition.
Printed in the United States of America.

Chinatown Christmas
(Chen Family Cuisine #1)

Kailin Gow

AUTHOR'S NOTE

Thank you for picking up Chinatown Christmas. This
is a full standalone book.

This series is a romantic comedy
recommended for age 18 and up and has adult
subject matter and language.

Summary

Food, family, and the passage of time have always gone hand in hand for the Chen Family, keeper of some of the most ancient recipes in time. It is rumored some of the cuisines created by the Chen's most secret recipes contained magic. For the three American-born Chen Sisters, the legendary secret recipes were just folklore until one by one, they began seeing something miraculous...

About Chinatown Christmas - "A Chinatown Christmas" refers to the saying that you can always find a restaurant open on Christmas day in Chinatown when all the other restaurants are closed.

Billionaire Jake Austin, has spent the last five years working through Christmas as he built his start up to a billion-dollar corporation. Every year, he's spent Christmas Day eating at the Chen Family Cuisine Restaurant, located in his local Chinatown down the street from his house. It was the only restaurant opened in town.

Every year, he always ate alone. Like the cold ruthless and arrogant billionaire that he was. Until this year, when someone decided to sit at his table.

******

Eldest daughter of the American-born Chen family in California, Charisma Chen has noticed the reclusive Jake Austin dine alone at her family's restaurant for years. Ever since he brutally berated her on her first day of work at his start up, she's kept her distance, even at her own family restaurant where she and her sisters would gather for Christmas every year to spend Christmas with her parents, who insisted on keeping the restaurant open even on Christmas Day.

This year, Charisma is going to close the restaurant for the first time on Christmas Day to give her parents a break. But for some reason, when Jake Austin shows up at the restaurant, something inside of Charisma makes her change her mind.

Something that has something to do with her past or was it something to do with the ancient folklore of the Chen Family Cuisine?

Prologue

<u>Charisma</u>

<u>Christmas Day 1 Year Ago</u>

There he was again. Alone, aloof, almost arrogant.

Once again hidden behind the large menu my father insisted on keeping, the lone man sat at a corner table of my family's Chinese restaurant.

After all, we were the only place open on this Christmas day. Many families, looking to get away from a night of cooking and washing dishes, came

7

in with their children, many with the grandparents, and all were smiling, happy and festive.

The lone man was uninterested in it all. Like every other year, he spoke to no one, looked at no one. He simply ordered, ate and left.

This year, I'd seen him walk in. Tall and lean, he held a stern expression in his deep blue eyes. His dark hair was kept short in the back while he had a tousle of curls above his brow. His style of dress was casual and lowkey. His dark gray slacks and plain blue shirt were a far cry from the crazy and silly Christmas sweaters many of the other patrons wore.

"Charisma," my father said, startling me as he came up from behind. "We've got mouths to feed. Why are you just standing there?"

"It's just so strange," I whispered, my eyes still on the lone man.

"Oh," my father said as he followed the direction of my gaze. "Him again. It is strange, isn't it?" he said with a chuckle. "Every Christmas."

"Yeah."

He turned his stern business eye to me. "Go see what he wants."

"Urgh," I let out.

There was something about him that was cold and unappealing. He was a Christmas downer. I felt chipper and happy and feared he would ruin that.

"Sure thing, Dad," I finally said.

For the past four years he'd been coming to the Chen Family Cuisine restaurant that my family ran. For the past four years, he arrived with a *just-another-Tuesday* expression on his face. For the past four years he sat at the same table, not speaking to anyone except to give his order.

Well, at least he had the courtesy to say thank you when served.

Two years earlier, when my dad decided to stop accepting cash, I'd learned that the lone man's name was Jake Austin. Or at least that's the name that appeared on his credit card.

I walked up to his table wondering if he was lonely. If I struck up a conversation, would he engage or rebuff?

Hmm. Was that stern look in his eyes due to his loneliness… or was it the reason he was always alone?

"Hello," I said as I reached his table. "Hello and merry Christmas."

He grunted.

"Would you like a bit more time to make your decision?"

"No," he said without lowering the menu one bit. "I'll have the number eight for one, no soup."

"Perfect." I reached out and took the menu away from him.

I looked into his face for the briefest moment. He really was a very good-looking man, despite the hard and unfriendly eyes. One could have easily mistaken him for a model or even an actor.

As I walked away, my mind's eye was filled with the image of his face. I couldn't help but wonder what he looked like when he smiled. Was he capable of smiling?

"A number eight for one," I called out when I reached the kitchen.

"Great." My younger sister, Sally, cried out as she walked in behind me. At twenty-four, she'd repeatedly shown her devotion to her work at the family restaurant. Smart and serious, she also tended to be on the shy side, making it at times difficult for her to go out and be among people.

"I get the family of twelve," she went on. "They ordered a number two for two, and number seven for one and a number one for… Oh, I don't even know anymore." She looked to our father with that pouting little face that usually got her what she wanted. "How come she gets the easy table?"

I smiled at her. "Don't be jealous, little sister. He might be alone, but he is the worst curmudgeon that you can imagine. Never says anything. Never even looks up when he orders. Like he's an Emperor or something. What's with that?"

"At least he's a generous tipper," Tammy, my youngest sister, said as she set various bowls of food on a large tray. At twenty, she didn't take her work at the restaurant very seriously, but being the baby of the family, she usually got away with it. "Last year I served him, and he left a pretty nice tip."

"You should know, Charisma," Sally said to me. "He's always sat in your section. Same table. Christmas Day. Every year. You're overworked with your studies for PhD, that you're just going through the motions of order taking, yourself. You've really never noticed the customers."

I laughed. "That's not true."

Chinatown Christmas
(Chen Family Cuisine #1)

"I agree," Tammy called out as she hoisted the heavy tray up to her shoulder level and headed for the door. "If you did, you'd notice he's close to your age, and pretty good-looking."

Sally sighed, "Like a hot book boyfriend from one of my favorite D.R. Love steamy books."

I shook my head. Sally was a hopeless romantic.

"You two leave your sister alone," Dad said, saying it loud enough to ensure that Tammy heard his comment as well. "She could have taken this day to relax or study… USC's Digital Technology program in the Annenberg graduate program mustn't be easy. She's the only one getting a doctorate in it. But instead, she came all the way down to Chinatown to help us out."

"Thanks, Dad," I said, happy to see that he recognized the sacrifice I was making.

"And," Dad went on, "if your sister wants to waste all her time paying attention to the handsome and clearly single man in the room, well that's her prerogative."

He winked at me, and my sisters burst out laughing.

"Dad," I whined.

I looked into his playful eyes. He and my mother worked so hard to make Chen's Family Cuisine, the family restaurant a success and yet he always managed to keep the atmosphere in the hectic and busy kitchen light and fun.

"Clay!" my mother shouted from the freezers at the back of the kitchen. "Stop chatting with the girls and come give me a hand with this!"

My father grinned and cocked his brow. "Right away, Dazzle. Right away."

Married for almost thirty years, my parents still have that twinkle in their eyes for each other. The perfect couple. It made me believe in romance, that there was someone out there for me like my mother had told me once before after my first breakup in high school.

Of course, having my parents' happy marriage set the standard for any romance of my own, I would envision my would-be future spouse to be someone quite like my father, jovial, easy-going, loved to cook, and a wonderful parent. Someone who would make me smile like my father has made my mother laugh and smile over the years.

Boy was I off.

Chapter 1

<u>Jake</u>

<u>*Thanksgiving Day – Present Day*</u>

This year, I gave into my mother's constant request for me to come back home for the holidays. So, I took a day off to fly out to my family home.

I looked at the spread my mom had prepared. Turkey, stuffing, mashed potatoes, sweet potatoes, stringed green beans, gravy and steaming hot biscuits. Thanksgiving in the Austin house was as traditional as traditional could be.

"You've barely touched my homemade stuffing, Jake," my mother said.

"Annie," my father said. "The boy just ate an entire drumstick, a mountain of mashed potatoes and three homemade biscuits with a pound of butter. Don't push him to eat more."

"It's not as if he can't stand to gain a pound or two," Mom grumbled.

Dad held his plate out to her. "How about giving me some of that famous homemade stuffing."

"Oh, William," she said with a pleased smile. "Anything to make me happy."

Dad winked at me as Mom spooned stuffing onto his plate.

"I still love your stuffing, Mom," I said as I brought my fork loaded with potatoes to my mouth. "I just prefer your mashed potatoes, that's all."

"All kidding aside," Dad said, giving me his wise-dad look. "You do look a little distracted."

"More than usual," Mom added.

I looked at them; the happily-married all American couple who worked hard, gave back to their community and kept a tidy but modest house. Their lives were happy and simple.

Not wanting to lay my business preoccupations on them, I shrugged. "You know how it is."

"Actually, no," Mom said.

It was difficult for either one of them to wrap their heads around what I really did for a living. At twenty-four, I had already started up and sold a successful tech company in San Francisco. I'd just as quickly begun work on YouBite and was now, only five years later, looking at the possibility of seeing that company go public.

"Dear," Mom said. "With you being so busy with… well, whatever it is that you're so busy with, we were wondering if you were planning on being home for Christmas this year."

The guilt rose up to my throat the way it did every year when I was away from home for the holidays.

Chinatown Christmas
(Chen Family Cuisine #1)

"I know that you're a big boy and these festivities aren't important to you like when you were a child," she went on. "But we put up a lovely tree, and we have a nice dinner and, of course, you can't have Christmas without a few traditional Christmas songs."

For the past five years, I'd stayed in Los Angeles during the holidays. I had so much work to do, so much to look into, so much that I wanted to get done…

"I'll try, Mom," I said. "I'll really try. But with YouBite about to go public… I have to keep a close eye on things and…"

"I understand, son," Dad said with a knowing grin. He gestured with his hands as if doing some sort of big business. "You're wheeling and dealing. You're making all that dough. Keep at it, son. I understand all the hard work that goes into making a business successful."

"Well, I don't, Will," Mom said as she shot her husband a disapproving glare. She turned to me with the same disapproving glare. "You already have more money than you know what to do with, Jake. How much happiness do you think these millions will bring you?"

"Billions, Mom," I corrected. "With the company going public, this will mean billions."

Completely unimpressed, she looked me square in the eye. "Well, look at that. My billionaire baby won't be coming home for Christmas… again."

"Mom," I groaned. I wanted to console her, but I knew that there was little that I could say.

Christmas had always been a big deal for her. And even if I was now older and had moved out of the family home, she still wanted the family together. It had always been important.

"You're going to be thirty soon," she said flatly.

I looked at her, my fork midway to my mouth. "So? What does that have to do with anything?"

"You're not getting any younger," she went on.

I shrugged and shot a knowing grin at my dad before bringing my gaze back to her. "No one is."

She set her fork down with a resounding clang. "I'm serious, Jake."

"Mom," I whined with a chuckle, trying to follow her logic. "What are you saying?"

"I'm saying that you're going to be thirty soon and all you ever think about is work. You don't have a girlfriend, you don't have a wife… and when in the world do you think you'll ever have children?"

Chuckling softly, I reached out to grasp her hand. "Are you looking forward to a few grandkids, Mom?"

Blushing, she looked at me and bit back on a smile. "Don't try to turn this on me. It's you that I'm concerned about. You know what they say about all work and no play."

"Mom," I said with a reassuring squeeze of her hand. "Don't worry. I take plenty of time off to… play. And I've dated plenty of girls over the years."

She pulled her hand free and looked at me with narrowed eyes. I knew she was going to come back at me with a solid argument. She always did.

Holding her hand in front of her face, her fingers up and outstretched waiting to be counted, she looked at me. "Let's see. And how many of those dates did we end up meeting?"

She looked at her hand and waited.

I had to laugh at the drama of it all.

"Oh, right," she said, letting her hand fall to the table. "None. Zero. Nada."

"I get it, Mom. No need to say it in every language."

"I just think that you're letting your best years pass you by," she went on.

"Mom, whether I'm at work or elsewhere, my best years are passing me by one way or another."

Raising her hands in the air in frustration, she glared up at the ceiling. "There you go again, always taking my words literally. You know what I mean. Do you really want to be fifty before becoming a father?"

"I promise you. I won't wait until I'm fifty."

"Look at your dad and me," she went on as she reached for his hand. "Right, Will? We've been together for how long… thirty? Thirty-two years?"

"Something like that," he said looking at her with a loving grin.

She looked back at me. "We have each other to lean on. We have each other to count on. You're not going to get that from casually dating one girl then the other."

I smiled at her. "I know that. Don't worry. When the right girl comes along, you'll be the first to know."

"Wrong," she said with a firmness that was uncharacteristic of her. "When the right girl comes along, you're going to be so preoccupied with making more and more money, that you're not even going to notice her. She'll simply walk past you and marry some other more deserving man."

I shrugged. "Then so be it."

Pressing her lips tightly together, she glared at my father and slapped his arm with the back of her hand.

"What?" he said with an innocent shrug.

"You did this," she said. "You raised him to think that this is okay. You've always pressed him to be a success and to make loads of money. Now, look at him. He is cynical and grumpy... and alone. What kind of woman is going to want that for a husband?"

Chinatown Christmas
(Chen Family Cuisine #1)

"Hey!" I let out, somewhat offended. "I'm still right here, Mom. What do you mean I'm cynical and grumpy? I'm an easy-going guy."

"As easy-going as Scrooge," Mom said. She threw her hands in the air as though making a wish and proclaimed, "Hopefully just once, just this Christmas, you'll find out how special, how wonderful Christmas really is."

Chapter 2

<u>Charisma</u>

<u>*Two Weeks Before Christmas - Present Day*</u>

Just before the holiday break from school, Professor Madison looked at me with pride. "I know that you've worked hard these past years, Charisma," he said. "As your supervising professor, I've watched you grow and come into your own."

"Thank you," I said. "It has been tough, but I'm glad I made it through."

"All you have left to do is your doctoral thesis."

Chinatown Christmas
(Chen Family Cuisine #1)

I nodded. My doctoral studies were finally over. "Just one little thesis to go and I'll get my Ph.D."

He nodded. "In June." He clasped his hands together. "In the meantime, you have until the holiday break and spring to get in that thesis. Put that time to good use."

"Oh, I will," I said before wishing him an early Happy Holidays as we left for break.

It was going to be a very fine balancing act. Not only did I have the thesis to work on, but I'd just nabbed a job in the product development department of a hotshot start-up called YouBite. In addition to that, I still planned on checking in on Chen Family Cuisine restaurant as often as possible. With YouBite conveniently located close to my family restaurant, I figured it would be easy to do both.

As I prepared for my first morning on the job starting on the first day of holiday break, I was a bundle of nerves. Despite getting up early and having set out my clothes the night before, I rushed as I took a quick shower, brushed out my hair then got dressed. Getting the job at YouBite wasn't that easy. I had to submit my grades, a bit of my work experience, and even conducted a Zoom interview with the hiring manager.

All that for a temporary job during the holiday season until Spring. Nevertheless, I felt excited to get an opportunity to put some of my studies into use at the tech start up. No matter how temporary it was. It may also provide me with the experience I needed to write my graduate thesis.

Not to mention, an excuse to dress up everyday in something other than sweats, t-shirts, and a hoodie, which was my go-to outfit as a graduate student.

Feeling cute yet professional in my sunny yellow dress and matching heels, I looked at my reflection. I smiled. I felt pretty… and ready to face whatever came my way.

All that was missing was a swipe of my signature red lipstick. Smacking my red lips together, I smiled at my reflection again.

Not bad.

As I made my way to the YouBite headquarters, I was once again struck by just how close the large building was to my family's restaurant in Chinatown. Keeping tabs on my family would be a pleasant noontime jaunt that I was sure to look forward to everyday. And with crime on the rise in Los Angeles, I really wanted to be there for my family.

With a spring in my step, I entered the large Gaudi inspired lobby. The space was endless, the ceilings sky high and every line was curved and delicious, almost sexy. The white tiled floor gleamed and the glossy white walls gave the impression of floating among the clouds.

A large oval, somewhat reminiscent of a flying saucer, sat in the center of the large space. In its center, the receptionist's desk.

"Hello," the receptionist said as I walked up to her. "Welcome to YouBite."

"Thank you," I said, looking all around me like a kid in a candy store.

The ceiling immediately above her went up five stories, the open hallways of the above floors visible from where she sat.

"This is such a beautiful place. What a wonder to work in."

The receptionist smiled patiently at me. "What can I do for you?"

"This is my very first day of work," I said.

"Oh," she said with a pleasant smile. "Welcome to the team. What's your name?"

"Charisma Chen."

Chinatown Christmas
(Chen Family Cuisine #1)

"Charisma Chen," the receptionist repeated as she opened the top drawer of her desk. "Yes. I have your ID card right here." She pulled out the silver card with the company logo on it. Beneath the logo was my name printed in blue. "Here you go."

I took the ID card and admired it for a long moment, repeatedly passing my finger over my name.

"You'll be working in product development, right?"

"That's right."

"That will be on the fourth floor." She stood and pointed to the right and behind her. "The elevators are right over there."

"Thank you," I said.

As I made my way to the elevator, I smiled and waved at the people as I passed them by. While their eyes all held a bewildered lack of recognition as they looked at me, they nonetheless waved back.

Rushing to an open elevator, I cried out, "Hold it."

But the doors closed. I quickly turned to see another elevator ready and waiting. I ran to it and as the doors began to close, I raised my leg in front of me hoping to stop the doors from closing. The doors jerked open, then began the process of closing again.

I hopped in, almost tripping in the process. Once inside the elevator, I lost my footing and toppled over, falling into the unsuspecting arms of the man standing there.

"Oh, no," I muttered, my face squished into the lapel of the man's elegant grey suit. "Oh, my God. I'm so sorry."

Pulling away from him as the elevator lurched up, I looked up at him with apologetic eyes.

"In a rush, are we?" he said, his tone anything but playful and forgiving.

Chinatown Christmas
(Chen Family Cuisine #1)

"I really am sorry. This is my first day and I didn't want to be late and…"

His jaw tight, he narrowed his eyes, and a vague hint of a sneer curved his lips. Confused, I looked at him. Okay, so I tripped and fell into him. But why so sour about it?

He glanced down and I followed his gaze.

"Oh, no," I muttered. "I'm so sorry."

A large, brown wet spot covered his thigh uncomfortably close to his crotch.

"Is that…?"

"Hot coffee," he growled. "Thanks to you and your rush to get to work on time, not only will I not have my morning coffee… not only will I have a burn on my thigh, but I will now be late for work."

Mortified, I quickly reached into my purse and pulled out a paper tissue and dabbed the wet spot.

"What are you doing?" he said as he grabbed my wrist and stopped my dabbing.

"Just trying to minimize damage, sir."

"By touching my crotch?" he said with a tight, hissing breath.

My heart jumped to my throat, and I stepped back.

"I assure you," he said. "You are not helping matters."

The anger in his eyes was gone, replaced with discomfort. He stood stiff for a moment, still holding my wrist.

"You should have a doctor look at that burn before it…"

"Fortunately for me, miss," he hissed, "I bought this coffee five minutes ago and it's had time to cool to where it is now leaving me with a warm, toasty feeling along my groin."

I smiled. "Oh, good. At least there's that."

He narrowed his eyes again and a mocking sneer clearly took control of his lips. "I should have you fired right this instant. It's your lucky day," he went on as the elevator doors opened. "I'm late for a meeting as it is, and I don't have time to deal with this."

I swallowed the ball of fear that'd lodged in my throat.

He stepped out of the elevator and turned to hold the doors open as he looked at me. With absolute disdain in his eyes, he looked me over. "Report to HR. Tell them that Jake Austin sent you."

Jake Austin? The Jake Austin who owns YouBite and my new boss? But not only that. Those unsmiling eyes. That tight jaw. It hit me why Jake Austin looks familiar. Not only is Jake Austin the owner of YouBite, but he's the same Jake Austin who's been coming to Chen's restaurant on Christmas for the past five years. That grump Jake Austin?

Dressed in a classy suit with his hair combed back and off his face, his appearance was even more austere and stern than on those Christmas nights that now came flooding back to me.

Numb, I stared at him. I barely recognized the man who would come in alone, sit alone in that corner table and eat his Christmas dinner all alone. I thought of all those times when I'd been concerned for him, feeling sorry for the lone man on Christmas day.

But looking at him now, I completely understood why he was always alone. Who would want to have Christmas dinner… or any other dinner for that matter, with such a grump?

Chapter 3

Charisma

After a few wrong turns, I finally found Human Resources and was greeted by a tall, beautiful redhead. Sitting elegantly behind her clear, glass top desk, her long legs crossed in a sensual manner, she was all business with a touch of femininity that I'd rarely seen before. Wearing a dark green wrap-around dress and mile-high stilettos, the woman exuded confidence almost to the point of arrogance.

Before I could even say a word to her, she looked up from the files on her desk and gave me a very scathing up and down glance.

"You must be Charisma," the redhead said, closing the folder on her desk and sitting back.

How d'you know? I wanted to say. Instead, I just stuck with, "Yes. Mr. Austin told me to come."

"Right," she said without the slightest hint of a smile. "I'm Cindy Marigold, HR manager."

I glanced sidelong at the chairs set up in front of her desk, expecting her to invite me to sit down.

She didn't, and I remained standing.

"I'm the new Product Development Scientist," I said. "Temporary, that is… for the winter break… until spring."

"Yes," Cindy said, looking at me from over the top of her stylish glasses. "I know. You're here to take over Janet's duties while she's out on maternity leave."

I shrugged. I had no idea who I was replacing or why.

"All right," Cindy said as she got up and came around her desk. "Come this way." She clucked her tongue as she passed by me and raised her chin in disdain.

I followed her out of her office and down a brightly lit hall. Our heels clip clopped on the shiny silver blue floor announcing our passage to everyone nearby.

As we passed a set of large double doors, Cindy pointed to them with relevance and respect. "That's Jake's office."

Oh, I thought. *Good to know.*

"And whose office is that?" I said, trying to make light conversation as we passed a pure white door.

"That's none of your concern."

I looked at her and forced a smile. How about another strategy. "Have you been working here long?"

"Long enough," she said haughtily.

We continued to clip clop our way down the hall in increasingly tense silence.

"And this is the research department," Cindy said as she dramatically pushed through a set of double doors.

Two researchers in white lab coats and thick protective goggles immediately stopped what they were doing and stood, almost at attention as they faced Cindy.

"Charisma Chen," Cindy said with biting formality. "This is Harold Pine, a USC grad and an assistant researcher here at YouBite."

The diminutive man pressed a dry grin, barely making eye contact with me.

"And that is Penny Richards, our lead researcher."

The heavy-set woman with thick glasses and her dark hair pulled back into a loose bun nodded.

"This," Cindy said, gesturing vaguely at me, "is Charisma Chen. She'll be replacing Janet, but don't worry. This is a temporary arrangement.

Janet will resume her duties here once her maternity leave is over."

Gee, thanks for the vote of confidence.

I momentarily glared at her and wanted to ask how I'd rubbed her the wrong way but turned to smile at my new team instead.

"Nice to meet you," Harold said with a curt nod.

Penny smiled with genuine excitement. "Welcome to the team."

Sensing that I might have finally met a friendly employee of YouBite, I smiled. "I can't wait to get started."

With the introductions complete, Cindy turned on her designer heel and headed for the door, stopping at the nearby shelf. "Oh, and by the way," she said as she grabbed a thick blue binder from the shelf. She turned to face me with a derisive grin on her lovely face. "You should take a look at that."

She handed the heavy book to me, and I looked down at the cover: YouBite Policy Handbook.

"You are to read it," Cindy said. "And you are expected to memorize it."

Frowning, I looked up at her. "Memorize it? This thing must be…" I flipped through the pages. With the font extra-large and the pages printed only on one side, there were well over a hundred pages. "I can't memorize all this. No one can."

Cindy looked at me with a cunning glare. "And yet it is Jake Austin himself who insists that you, Charisma Chen, read, learn and memorize every point in that handbook."

Jake? Was this his way of getting back at me for spilling coffee on him?

"But…"

Walking to the door, she glanced back at me. "It's up to you. Just be warned…" she went on as she flipped her long auburn locks over her shoulder and turned to me. "Jake Austin isn't one of those bosses who is always flying around the world. He is very present here at the YouBite headquarters. There is a high probability that you will one day run into him. When that day comes, he will no doubt ask for your view on Rule 18-a, or ask for your opinion on Rule 23-c. Or he might just ask you to completely recite Rule 3-d. If you fail to give him an appropriate view, a comprehensive opinion or simply fail to recite the entirety of a rule, you will be fired."

I wanted to laugh with incredulity. I wanted to guffaw at the absurdity. Was this a joke? Was this some juvenile initiation? It had to be. It couldn't possibly be real.

I looked to Harold and Penny for confirmation that it was all a joke. Penny cast her gaze down to the immaculate floor and blushed, clearly embarrassed. Harold, on the other hand, sneered, his brow cocked in anticipation of my failing to prove myself.

Did I exude incompetence? Was the request to learn this handbook proof that I'd done something wrong?

Crossing his arms over his scrawny chest, Harold raised his chin, exposing the vulnerability of his neck. A clear sign that he saw me neither as a threat or a competent boss. His sneer deepened.

He was so easy to read. Too easy. While I had a talent for reading people and was highly intuitive, any amateur could see the resentment and disdain in every line on his face.

He disliked me.

Wishing to read him better, I tried to catch his gaze. His eyes, eyes of a conspirator, were fixed on Cindy.

"I'll leave you three to get acquainted," Cindy said as she walked out.

At her departure, I tried to read deeper into Harold, to get to the depths of his thoughts.

Chinatown Christmas
(Chen Family Cuisine #1)

I'd recently learned that I had the capacity to do so. The Chen genealogy tree was dotted with psychics of various levels. Some could only intuit the feelings of others while others clearly read every single thought that passed through someone's mind.

One or two members of the Chen generally had this talent in every generation. While I knew that I was fortunate enough to be one of them, the other was still a mystery, although I strongly suspected that Tammy or Sally might be the other candidate. Definitely Dazzle, my mother.

Discretion was the order of the day, and it was something that was not talked about. It just exists.

I also had yet to discover the depths of my ability and wished to test it out on Harold, but my attention turned to Penny.

"It's always a good thing when we have another woman on the team," Penny gushed. "I can't wait to work with you."

I smiled, quickly reading her genuine eagerness to get to know me.

I looked at them both, hoping to convey not only my friendliness, but my desire to work with them and be a good and efficient supervisor.

"So," I said. "What are we working on?"

Harold immediately turned away from me. "*We*," he said with sarcastic emphasis, "are not working on anything. *I*, however, have work to get to."

He walked away, returning to his work station that was in the far corner of the large lab room.

"Don't mind him," Penny said. "He takes his work very seriously and sometimes that makes him seem… well… He really is a good guy underneath it all."

I smiled at her but didn't believe her for a second. "I'll take your word for it." I clasped my hands together and hauled in a good, long breath. "Now, where do I get started?"

Penny looked sheepishly at me. "I wish I could help you. I have my nose in a petri dish pretty much of the time and don't really raise my head often to see what's going on."

"Janet's desk is over there," Harold shouted from the corner. "If you two could stop yakking, I've got some serious work to do and I need all my concentration, thank you very much."

Penny shrugged and whispered. "Come on. It's right over there."

Janet's desk was a blank slate. Aside from a computer screen, a phone and a large brightly colored plastic molecule, the desk was spotless.

My first blemish on the pristine white desk was the dreaded policy handbook that I pushed to the far corner of the desk. Then I set my purse over the edge of the chair and pulled the chair back to sit down. Pulling open one drawer after the other, I looked for clues as to what I should do.

Nothing.

Then I slid out the keyboard that was tucked under the desk and tried to get the computer going. I was immediately prompted to enter a password.

"Great." I glanced at the policy handbook and flipped idly through the pages. "I bet this thing doesn't have something useful to tell me like what the password here would be, right?"

"Janet has a cat named Pickles," Penny said. "I'd be willing to bet that that's the password."

"I'll give it a try." I typed in pickles.

Nothing.

"Any other ideas?" I said.

"Did you put a capital 'p'?"

Right. I typed it in again, this time capitalizing the 'p' and... voila! The screen turned on and welcomed me to YouBite.

Chinatown Christmas
(Chen Family Cuisine #1)

"Thanks," I said, looking up at Penny. "For a girl who doesn't really know what's going on around here, you're very helpful."

"Glad I could help," she said, biting the corner of her lip. "But now I have to go back to my own work. We're running late as it is."

"Oh," I said before she could walk away. "Could you just let me know what it is that you're working on?"

She shrugged. "Our latest product, and it's set to launch on New Year's day."

I nodded my understanding.

"But they want a soft launch the day after Christmas." She shrugged. "They tell us that it's why we can't take Christmas off. This thing has to be ready on time. It's the biggest product launch period and they want to take full advantage of that."

Harold got up from his workstation and came to us. At first I feared he would berate us, but with his hands on his hips, he stopped beside Penny, seemingly eager to take part in the conversation.

"If you must know, Christmas has been the same for years now. It's one product launch after the other. And since they always do well, Mr. Austin wishes to uphold that tradition. And that is why he has such faith in his team. We always do well, and we will do well again this year." He looked at Penny. "And the reason we can't take Christmas off is that Mr. Austin is a perfectionist, and he wants to ensure that we are putting every available minute into making his products perfect."

I chuckled. "So you guys are sort of like Santa's little elves."

Penny giggled while Harold glared at me with unwarranted disgust.

"Well," Harold said in his haughty manner. "If that is the level of banter we can expect, I'll get back to my enzymes."

As he walked away, Penny and I exchanged amused glances. We were on the same wavelength.

Chinatown Christmas
(Chen Family Cuisine #1)

"I'll get back to work," she said.

And I turned to my computer to figure out where to go from there. Opening one file after another, I tried to figure out the direction the company was going in.

Messages were cryptic and documents were intentionally vague. There were orders for various items; chemical elements, preservatives, and comestible ingredients.

"What is the big secret that no one wants to talk about?" I whispered to my computer screen.

Then I came upon an internal letter:

Due to the highly competitive nature of the industry that we are delving in, it is imperative that employees remain on a need-to-know basis. The desired final product must be known only to authorized personnel.

With that in mind, please ensure that individuals in the research department only receive materials pertinent to their specified task in the development of this product.

YouBite wishes to distance itself from its competitors in every conceivable way. YouBite is unique. YouBite is innovative. YouBite always keeps everyone guessing.

And this year, YouBite will launch something truly amazing.

What will YouBite come up with now? That is the question that everyone will want to hear the answer to.

Let's strive to make it worth their while.
Thank you,
Management

Gee. What was YouBite working on that could possibly so secretive?

Each document that I opened and read brought me a little closer to the answer.

Chinatown Christmas
(Chen Family Cuisine #1)

Finally, it was there, in black and white.

YouBite was entering an arena that I knew an awful lot about.

Food.

Chapter 4

Looking up from my computer, I realized that Harold and Penny were gone.

Had they said goodbye?

I shrugged, but then noticed the time. Five past nine.

My stomach suddenly rumbled loudly, reminding me that I hadn't had dinner. I gathered my things and prepared to leave. As I grabbed my purse, my phone rang.

"Hi, Mom," I said, seeing her name on my screen as I answered.

"Honey, where are you? I thought you said that you would stop by after work."

Chinatown Christmas
(Chen Family Cuisine #1)

"Sorry, Mom," I said, hugging the phone between my chin and shoulder as I continued to pick up my belongings. "I'm still at the office."

"Oh, Charisma. It's past nine o'clock. What are you still doing there?"

"First day on the job, Mom," I said as I walked out of the lab and locked up. "I had a lot of things to learn, but I'm finished now. I'm walking out the door as we speak."

"Then come on over and have dinner."

"Now? Mom. It's late."

"It's never too late. We're waiting for you."

I chuckled. "Okay, Mom. I'm on my way."

Rushing down the deserted hall with the deafening echo of my steps in my ears, I came to an abrupt stop when I saw light coming from under Jake's office. Curious to know if he was really still at the office, I took a step closer to the door and heard him talking on the phone.

The guy is a real workaholic, I thought as I reached out to touch the door hoping to connect to his thoughts.

Nothing. I lay my palm flat on the oak door.
Still nothing.

That's strange. It was almost as if something was blocking my psychic attempt.

Shrugging, I gave up and walked away. Well, I thought as I boarded the elevator, at least there's little chance of my running into him if he's so busy.

Down at the lobby of the huge building, I crossed the path of a few other diligent workers, then headed out to the well-lit parking lot.

No need to worry about finding my car in the vast lot. It sat there, all alone in the second section of the lot.

The drive to my family's restaurant was quick and easy and the heavenly scents of delicious food immediately had my tastebuds eager for a bite.

Chinatown Christmas
(Chen Family Cuisine #1)

"We were just about to give up on you," Tammy said as she finished clearing a table.

"Sorry I made you guys wait," I said. I headed straight to the kitchen and went up to my mother to kiss her cheek.

Dad was busy stirring up vegetables while Sally was right beside him, watching every move he made. I knew it was important that she learn every family recipe. She was the one who wanted to carry on running the family restaurant long after my parents retire, if they ever would retire.

Unlike me and my youngest sister Tammy, having opted not to go to college, Sally was the ideal candidate to learn everything there was to know about running the family restaurant and keeping the ancient family recipes alive.

"Come give us a hand," Dad said.

Me? I wanted to say. I was exhausted from my day at YouBite and had little interest in cooking anything.

"Yes, you," Mom said with a knowing grin.

Dad looked at all of us as he flicked his pan up to flip over the vegetables inside. "I know that we told you girls that we'd only be training Sally," he said. "But your mother and I have decided that it's best that all three of you learn the family recipes."

"Dad," I said, wanting to argue the point but knowing better.

"This is too important," Dad said. "Every single one of these ancient family recipes must be preserved. They must be passed down." Setting his pan aside, he turned to look at us. "And we are now going to pass them down to you."

"Tammy," Mom said. "Did you lock the door?"

"Yes."

"Did you put up the 'closed' sign?"

Chinatown Christmas
(Chen Family Cuisine #1)

With a huff and lazy arms flapping at her sides, she left the kitchen.

I turned to my dad. "I appreciate the need to do this, Dad, but I've had a really long day."

Growing uncharacteristically solemn, he looked at me, his eyes stern and uncompromising. "This shall be done… tonight."

He turned to a locked pantry and unlocked it. "You girls are now old enough to see this and to understand its importance."

He opened the pantry door and pulled out an ornate mahogany box that looked to be well over a hundred years old.

Setting it on the counter, he then turned the ring on his finger so that it was palm down and set the ring over the locking mechanism of the ancient box.

I had long ago noticed the beautiful gold ring with the clover scroll design. I had even asked my father the origin of the ring, but he'd always been evasive.

Now I understood why.

The top of the box popped open. Inside was a large leather-bound book with the Chen name on it.

With reverence, he took the book out of the box and held it in his hands for a long moment. "You girls must never forget the importance of this book."

He looked at Sally. "Right?"

Having seen the book many times before, she nodded. Even Tammy knew of the book.

In awe of the power and the history of the ancient book, I reached out to touch it.

Smiling, my father pulled the book away. "Your pursuits led you in another direction, dear daughter, and I respect that. We all do. I'm sure that with your time spent on your studies, and now this new job, you thought that you'd be exempt from learning about all this. Unfortunately, that cannot be so."

"Well," Sally went on. "With crime being what it is these days, you never know. Then you have pandemics to think about and climate change and mental health…"

"Okay, I get it. Things are bleak," Tammy said.

"God forbid anything should ever happen to any of you," Mom said. "You are all smart, strong women and I have faith in all of you. But we realize that it was unwise to limit the knowledge in this book to only one child. We have three children, and each will learn. It is your heritage, your right and your responsibility."

Dad set the book on the counter and opened it. "You'll notice that the recipes appear to be like any other gourmet Chinese dish. We have things like dumplings, roast duck, rice and stir-fried vegetables. The secret, however, is in the special ingredients that are in each and every recipe."

He backed away from the book and, with a gesture of his hand, invited us to take a closer look. "I want each of you to choose a dish or two and we'll get started."

The next hour was a flurry of activity as we all adopted a special recipe and took to the task of successfully completing it.

"Don't forget to keep stirring," Dad said as he came up behind me.

He moved onto Tammy. "You want them to be tender, but not mushy," he said of her vegetables.

"I know, I know, Dad," Sally said as he made his way to her side. "Don't manipulate the dough too much. It'll make it tough and stringy."

He smiled and patted her back. "You are all doing very well. I'm proud of all of you."

We soon completed our dishes and brought everything to the small round table set at the back of the kitchen.

Chinatown Christmas
(Chen Family Cuisine #1)

There, in the midst of all the pots and pans, the bags of rice, the potted fresh herbs, we sat together and enjoyed a family meal.

"Charisma," Mom said between bites. "How was your first day at… what's the name again?"

"YouBite," I said, happy to talk about my day. "It was really exciting. You should see the interior of this building. It's awesome. I don't even understand how the thing stays standing. It curves here and there, and I'm sure that I'll end up getting lost, but for today, I made it to my office without…" I hesitated. "… without incident."

Mom looked at me with those knowing and wise eyes. "And these two men who are putting obstacles in your way. Tell us about them."

Popping an entire dumpling in my mouth, I pointed to my puffed cheeks as I stalled to give an answer. How did she know there were two men at YouBite that made my first day not so pleasant? She

63

was far too intuitive for me to try to steer away from the question. Of course, she was also psychic.

"No need to be embarrassed, dear," Mom said, patting my hand. "Please share with us your experience."

I swallowed my dumpling, cleared my mouth of any remnants and propped my elbows on the table. "You're right, Mom," I said. "Two of the men that I ran into seemed unhappy to see me there, and I have no idea why. But I'm sure that, in time, they will come around. I'm confident that I can change their minds and make them see that I have a place in that company."

"Over-confidence can sometimes be your worst enemy, Charisma. While I have faith in your ability to bring people over to your side, don't underestimate some people's desire to remain cold and unwelcoming. But you've always been the sunny one, always so optimistic and positive."

I grinned. "Thanks., Mom. I knew you'd agree with me."

Chinatown Christmas
(Chen Family Cuisine #1)

"Well," Dad said as he pushed his plate away slightly. "As good as this is, I can't eat another bite."

"Good," I let out.

Surprised, everyone looked at me.

Smiling, I shrugged as I got up and grabbed a few to-go containers from the cabinet. "I was thinking about my new boss. He was still at work when I left and I'm willing to bet that he hasn't had dinner yet."

I spooned rice into a container and dumplings into another.

"Oh," Sally said. "Isn't that cute. She's going to prepare dinner for her boss. How very sweet of you."

I playfully glared at her. "Not only that, little sister, but I will personally deliver this dinner myself. YouBite is just a couple of blocks away."

"Good," Mom said. "Our last delivery was half an hour ago and Benjamin left right after that."

"Well," I said. "I wouldn't want to bother Benji with this delivery anyway. He already works hard enough."

I carefully packed the containers into a thick paper bag and rolled up the top.

"I'll catch you all tomorrow," I said as I left them and made my way back to YouBite.

My nerves caught up with me the minute I drove into the parking lot and looked at the front entrance of YouBite. How would Mr. Austin react to my special delivery? Hopefully it'll make him forget about that unfortunate incident with his coffee spill this morning.

"We'll soon find out," I told myself as I left my car, now parked only a few yards from the entrance.

The night guard on the other side of the glass door stood and came to look straight at me with a what-do-you-want shrug.

Chinatown Christmas
(Chen Family Cuisine #1)

I held up my new ID card. "I left something in my office."

He looked carefully at my ID card, then gestured to my paper bag.

"I need to drop this off for the staff tomorrow morning," I lied.

Without smiling, he nodded and unlocked the door. "You have ten minutes."

"Okay," I said as I rushed to jump on the waiting elevator.

My heart rate increased as the elevator went up and the doors opened. Walking lightly, I made my way to the boss's door with the intention of leaving the take-out bag on the floor, knocking on the door and running.

But the moment I reached the door, it swung open, and Jake stood there looking straight at me.

While I was startled and caught off guard, he was not surprised at all to see me standing there at his door.

"I…" I said, holding the bag out to him. "I just thought that you might be hungry and… I mean… earlier…" I pointed in the direction of the lab where I'd worked all day. "I noticed as I left that you were still here and… well, I thought… you know… it's so late… and…"

Expressionless, he looked at me, took a step forward and took the proffered bag of food.

Nodding, he unrolled the top of the bag and looked inside. "Nice." He looked back at me. "You're the girl from earlier this morning."

I cocked an innocent brow.

"You spilled my morning coffee all over my three-hundred-dollar slacks. And they're my favorite. I suppose that this is your way of trying to make up for that."

"Well," I dared to say. "Actually, I just thought you'd be hungry, and I thought you'd be happy to have a nice, hot meal after such a hard day at work."

Scrunching up his face in displeasure, he nodded. "You know, if I wanted to order food, I'm very capable of doing so myself."

Surprised by his sour reception of my hand delivered dinner, I poked my tongue into my cheek and held back from calling him a full-blown grump.

"But," he said. "While I have you… why don't you tell me the first rule in the Employee Policy Handbook."

Damn. Really?

I looked sheepishly at him then mustered up my brightest and most optimistic smile. "Don't spill coffee on your boss?"

He took a firm step closer until his face was so close to mine that I can see the gold flecks in his hazel eyes which made them almost gold. I was mesmerized for a moment, lost in those golden eyes.

Damn, he was handsome. His eyes were piercing but friendly at the same time, and fringed with dark long lashes that any woman would be jealous of. He had thick dark eyebrows that had a natural arch which gave him a rakish air of arrogance. Chisel cheeks, an aristocratic nose, and full lips along with his dark thick almost windswept-looking hair along with the black cashmere sweater he had changed into for the night, gave him the tortured look of a suffering lord who lived in some gothic castle hidden away on a moor somewhere in England.

He looked down on me like some arrogant lord. "That usually goes without saying. Everyone who works here knows not to do that without having to put it into a handbook." His tone was harsh and condescending.

I struggled to swallow the uncomfortable ball lodged in my throat. Was he going to fire me right there on the spot? After all, that's what Cindy had said.

"I'll give you another try," he said, his voice so deep and sinister that a chill ran up my spine.

"Wardrobe restrictions?"

Shaking his head, he started to walk away. "Wrong again. I strongly suggest you read that handbook tonight, and I suggest you memorize every point in that book. Who knows when I'll try to test you again." His eyes swept over me, from head to toe and then back up again until they stopped at my lips. "If you fail again, I might have to punish you."

I swallowed. Why did that sound so sexy?

Nearing the elevators, he glanced over his shoulder. "You have to know it by heart."

And he was gone, leaving me standing there alone and completely bewildered.

Chapter 5

It took me a minute to gather my wits, But I made it home and fell into bed immediately, out like a light.

I dreamt of myself in a manor house out on the moors, dressed in a beautiful chiffon and silk dress while it is pouring rain outside, the wind screaming through a storm. The door opens, and Jake Austin, wearing tights that hugged his muscular legs, thighs, and buttocks along with a jacket that covered his wide chest and shoulders like Heathcliff in Wuthering Heights bursts through the door. He sees me and rushes over to grab me before he bends me over for a deep passionate kiss. He's soaking wet, which soaks through my dress as well.

Chinatown Christmas
(Chen Family Cuisine #1)

Soon he's fumbling through my dress as we slid down to the ground and begin doing more than just kissing.

And more action than I've ever had before.

Whew!

I woke up the next morning sweaty and my sheets soaking wet as though I was caught in a downpour.

My hand went up to my mouth in surprise. There was no way I could have sweated that much to soak my sheets like that. No way that I could have been in an actual downpour. Or with someone who had been in a downpour.

But then again, I did have a dish I made last night from the ancient family cookbook. A dish I called, Make Your Dream Come True Dumplings. Which I also gave Jake last night.

Oh my goodness. Did the dumplings I ate really made my dream seem so real that it became real?

No, it couldn't be. But then again, there was something so special and even magical about our family's ancient recipes. That was why it was so important to guard them and to pass it down to the next generation.

But last night's hot dream with Jake? If that was ever true, how could I face him, especially after everything we did in that dream?

Well, there was one way to find out and that was to go into work. Sexy hot dream aside, I was raring to go. Despite the late night at the office and cooking dinner at the restaurant with my family, I was eager to really dive into my work.

Feeling pretty and flirty in my lacy orange sheath dress, I arrived at YouBite early, so early that aside from the guard at the entrance, I didn't cross the path of any other employees.

Chinatown Christmas
(Chen Family Cuisine #1)

And, once up on my floor, I noticed that, once again, the light was on in Jake's office. Then I heard his stern voice, already on the phone with a supplier or buyer or whoever else he dealt with.

It was admirable to say the least. The man had enough money to simply sit back on some exotic beach sipping margueritas all day, but no. I did manage to look him up last night before I fell asleep, and learned he was a business prodigy who sold his first business about seven years ago that made him a billionaire. After selling off his first business, he took some years off before starting YouBite from scratch.

From my graduate studies, I figured he fit the profile of the tech CEOs which meant, he wasn't just running a company for profit, but for something he believed in. He was in his office working just as hard, if not harder than anyone else, which set an example of a strong work ethic at YouBite.

I arrived at the lab to find that my team wasn't there yet either. Good. I was looking forward to a bit of time alone to get my bearings. I headed straight for my desk, turned on the computer and got to work.

The first order of the day was outlining a little speech for a meeting with my staff. I wanted to make it clear to them who I was, what I wanted to achieve at YouBite and what I expected of them. I wanted to be brought up to date on the projects at hand and not waste any time.

By the time Harold arrived, my speech was complete. All that was left was to re-read it and make a few corrections.

You're still here?

I raised my head at the snide remark. Standing beside his workstation, he glared at me, drumming his fingers atop his desk.

I thought for sure that after one look at all the work in front of a little snit like you, you'd go running home to your mommy.

Chinatown Christmas
(Chen Family Cuisine #1)

Clenching my jaw, I stood and walked over to him, ready to give him a piece of my mind. If he thought that I was too young for the job, he was wrong. And if he thought that I was too weak for the job, he was definitely wrong. And if he thought that a heavy workload was going to scare me off, he was dead wrong.

But as my lips parted, ready to berate him and tell him who Charisma Chen was, I realized that he'd not spoken those words aloud at all.

I'd inadvertently read his thoughts… as bleak as they were.

With his defiant chin jutted out, he clasped his hands in front of him. In fact, I could have almost sworn that it was a protective move as he put his hands in front of his genitals.

Was I more of a threat to him than he wanted to let on?

"Good morning, Harold," I said, friendly, chipper, but clearly holding my own. "Happy to see you again."

He opened his mouth to speak, but I continued.

"You'll be happy to learn that I've had time to look over Janet's notes and the moment Penny arrives we'll have a little meeting and make sure that we're all on the same page."

"Actually, I have a lot of work to…"

Penny arrived and I immediately turned to her, ignoring Harold.

"Oh, good," I said. "We're all here. Like I was telling Harold, I'd like to have a little meeting with you two."

"Cool," Penny said. She tossed her handbag on her workstation and turned her attention back to me.

"I've set up two chairs in front of my desk," I said as I turned to head back to my corner of the lab. "So, let's settle in over here and have a nice little chat."

"I don't really have the…" Harold argued.

"Now, Harold," I said, pulling out the full force of my commanding voice.

Reaching my desk, I turned to invite them to each take a seat. Still bitter, Harold yanked back his chair and fell into it, immediately crossing his arms over his chest.

Penny and I exchanged knowing glances. She sat down and smiled.

As we chatted about YouBite and the upcoming product launch, Penny responded with a very open spirit, helping me out in every way possible.

Where Harold was tightlipped, Penny told me everything she'd been doing over the past months. Where Harold refused to bring any of his research to me, Penny offered me the entirety of her files and results.

Two hours into the meeting, despite Penny's help, I was still in the dark as to the exact nature of the project at hand. I suspected that Harold held the other part of the puzzle, the part that he was determined to keep secret.

"Thank you so much Penny for all your help." I looked at Harold who pressed his lips tightly together, a childish sign of defiance at best. "However, it's not enough, and I will now have to look into inviting the founder and owner of YouBite into the mix."

Harold grimaced. "Really? You think that Mr. Jake Austin, with all the responsibilities of running a huge corporation like YouBite, is going to take time out to come fulfill the curiosity of a little snit like you. Ha! You're even more naïve than you let on."

The door to the lab opened and in walked Jake. Damn he looked good. I couldn't help but think back to those steamy moments with Jake in my dream. Which seemed so real. And now what else? As if I dreamed of having Jake come to me at my beck and call, did eating those Make Your Dream Happen Dumplings still have an effect on me? Had I summoned Jake without even realizing it?

I smiled at Harold. "Well, well, well. Let's ask the man himself what he thinks of all this."

Harold fidgeted in his chair, shifting over to one butt cheek as he crossed his legs, clasped his hands together and poked his tongue into his cheek.

Jake stood there, large, hot in a black shirt and jeans, looking as arrogant and angry like Heathcliff again from Wuthering Heights.

"What are you all doing there?" Jake said as he came to my desk. Clearly confused, he looked at Penny, then Harold then back to me. "Is this your way of ensuring that everything is ready to go for

Christmas day? I mean, you are aware that the Christmas Day Project… as the name would indicate, is anticipated for…? You guessed it… Christmas day!"

Glaring at me, he set his fists on his hips and awaited an answer.

Calmly and completely in control of my emotions, I set my palms atop my desk and slowly rose to face him. "Thank you for stopping by my lab, Mr. Austin."

He cocked a brow, no doubt ready to argue the 'my lab' phrasing.

"Indeed," I said. "With Christmas just around the corner, I'm eager to ensure that the project is brought to completion by that time. That is why I've decided to sit with my team and enquire about the status of the project. However, I am still largely in the dark as to what the project actually is, and believe, as supervisor to this particular project that it is vital that I be kept abreast of everything that is going on."

Jake looked at Penny and Harold. "Well.." he said, gesturing with his hand that they speak up.

"I gave her all I have," Penny said.

"And you," he said, looking to Harold.

"Oh, of course," Harold said, strangely submissive all of a sudden. "It's no secret that Janet had me begin this project. As we speak, I am in the midst of getting the logistics down. Once that is complete, we'll move on with development."

"How far in the *midst* are you?" Jake said.

"About halfway," Harold said.

"And how many vendors have signed up for the launch so far?" Jake said.

Harold instantly looked to the floor prompting Jake to turn to Penny.

She shrugged. "Sorry. None."

"None?" Incredulous, he took a step back. "Are you kidding me?"

"I'll make sure that we'll get right on it," I said, hoping to reassure him.

"Damn right, we'll get right on it," he said as he rolled up his sleeves. He pulled up a chair and brought it up beside mine.

Confused, I looked at him, wondering what he was up to.

"Sit down and let's go through the vendor list," he said. "You do have the vendor list on that computer, don't you?"

I sat down and pulled up the list.

Jake looked to Penny and asked if she also had a copy of the list. She looked through her folder and pulled out a stack of stapled sheets of paper.

"Here you go," Penny said, handing him the list.

Jake looked through the list. "Just so you know," he said as he continued to peruse through the list. "This is so important that I am putting aside my own work in order to get this ready to launch on Christmas Day. You guys are way behind."

"Yeah, but…" Harold said.

"And don't try to blame Janet's maternity leave," Jake spat before Harold could finish his sentence.

Harold turned beet red and scrunched up his face.

"While I continue to go through this, you guys work on the logistics. I want this done within the next two days."

Jake and I went through the list while Harold and Penny worked out the logistics. After lunch Jake left with the list, leaving me to help out with logistics.

It was a long, exhausting day.

"I've done all I can with this," Penny said as she handed me the work she'd done. "I'm heading out."

"Already?" I said as I checked the time. "Damn. Sorry. I didn't realize that it was already five o'clock."

"See you tomorrow," she said as she left.

Harold, as expected, simply slammed his work onto the corner of my desk and left without saying a word.

I opened Harold's folder and went through it. At first I thought that I was reading it all wrong, but then realized that he was the one who had it all wrong. There was such a long series of errors that it was difficult to believe that he knew what he was doing.

I spent an hour correcting one line after the other, shaking my head all the way.

"What are you thinking, Harold?" I said as I cleaned up the mess that was his proposal.

"Who are you talking to?"

Startled, I jumped back from my desk and looked to the door of the lab where Jake was peeking in. Even with his hair a little disheveled, and him dressed down into casual wear, he was strikingly handsome.

"Sorry," he said as he opened the door fully and came in. "I didn't mean to scare you there."

I was taken aback. He was actually not so scary. Not even grumpy, but nice.

"I'm sorry," I said, quickly getting to my feet. "We've worked on this all day and there's still so much to do."

"I know," he said with a crooked smile. "That's why I brought this." He set the pizza box that he held onto the corner of my desk. "Figured I owed you one."

Whoa. What happened between yesterday and tonight?

Did he eat that Make Your Dreams Come True Dumplings or whatever it was called, and had that same dream I did? You know, the steamy one?

I tried to get a read on him, especially his thoughts but drew a blank. Why was he so hard for me to read?

Jake smiled a devastatingly dazzling smile. He wasn't just handsome. He was hot. He then reached into his pockets and pulled out two cans of soda, setting one down by me, the other closer to him.

"That sure smells good," I said as I opened the pizza box. I pulled out a hot, saucy slice and brought the point to my drooling mouth. "Oh," I let out as I chewed on the perfect pizza. "This is even better than it smells."

Jake's golden eyes dropped from my eyes to my lips as I licked my lips.

He closed his eyes for a brief moment, as though he was trying to control himself. *From what?*

"I'm starved," he muttered as he sat down in the chair that he'd brought up to my desk earlier and grabbed a slice. I wanted to comment on his softened and almost pleasant demeanor but feared it might awaken the angry beast he'd so far shown himself to be.

I popped open my can of soda and took a sip. "It's a good thing that we looked into the status of this project. Logistics are not what they should be."

Chomping on his slice of pizza, he nodded.

As I reached for a second slice of pizza, I glanced at him. "Thanks for this by the way. I hadn't realized just how hungry I was."

"I see," he said, his eyes dropping to my lips again. He kept staring until I poked out my tongue to see if I had anything on my lips.

I did.

Jake grabbed a napkin and wiped my lips.

My heart fell. So he *was* looking at my lips because it was messy. Not because he maybe felt something.

"So," he said through his chewing. "How much of the handbook have you memorized so far?"

Glancing up at him, I was about to smile, thinking he was joking, but his stern gaze left me livid.

"You have memorized it, right?"

I shook my head.

Really?

Fearing the worst, I looked at him and detected the faintest hint of a smile.

We brought the conversation back to the product launch and the logistics of it all. He listened intently to what I had to say and seemed to appreciate my perspective. We exchanged ideas, and I was surprised when he graciously accepted my criticism of one of his ideas.

"You're right," he said. "I hadn't thought of it that way. Good catch."

I smiled, enjoying the moment.

Could his pleasant disposition be due to the special meal I'd brought him the night before?

After all, the recipe that I had worked on from the Chen Family Recipe Book was meant to bring harmony and peace to all who shared in the dish.

Yeah, and I forgot that I had added some of those special dumplings into his carry-out bag as well.

Then again, I'd liked to think that my sunny personality and positive attitude towards everyone and everything was rubbing off on him.

After all, how could anyone remain grumpy when such a brilliant ray of sunshine warmed their souls?

Maybe it was both.

Chapter 6

<u>Jake</u>

Charisma. An interesting name for a woman who'd quickly found a way to get under my skin. What kind of name was that? So positive, divinely cheerful, and charming. While I had no doubt that her bright and bubbly personality was appreciated by those who knew her, somehow… it all just rubbed me the wrong way.

Who could be so upbeat, kind, and sweet?

Then again… intriguing. Beautiful and even sexy. Those pouty lips, long flowing wavy hair and curvaceous body was meant to belong to a seductress. A sorceress.

Despite working late into the night on the logistics that Harold had completely fucked up, I headed to the YouBite headquarters bright and early the next day.

Straying from my usual route, I veered off the highway and got in line for the drive-thru service of a local doughnut shop.

"Two large coffees, and two bagels with cream cheese on the side, please."

Two coffees? I thought as I waited for my order to be handed over. *Why two coffees?*

Charisma? I shrugged as I was handed the bag of bagels and the two large coffees.

Trying to think through the effect she had on me, I drove to work and was happy to see that there were no cars parked in front of the building. Once again, I was first to arrive.

Good, I thought as I got out of my car, grabbed my bagels and coffee and headed inside.

There was something soothing and calming about being the first to enter the building. Something about the serenity of the large space that was silent until the cavernous space echoed with the voices of my employees as they arrived.

I took the elevator; more silence and serenity.

I got off and headed to the lab to leave a coffee and bagel on Charisma's desk. No doubt she'd be pleased by the thoughtful gesture. Imagining seeing her face break into a happy smile, made the corners of my lips lift a bit.

When did I care about making someone smile?

Reveling in the solitude of walking through the space that I'd designed, that I'd helped build and that I was so proud of, I smiled and even dared to whistle a whimsical melody.

Damn. Whistle? Me?

Chinatown Christmas
(Chen Family Cuisine #1)

I wanted to ignore the way my thoughts repeatedly reverted back to Charisma; her bright smile, her optimistic and cheery gaze, the pleasant lilt of her voice… not to mention a very attractive fashion style that was a cheerful blend of sassy, sexy and classy. There was something regal about her, as though she came from royalty.

As I arrived at the door to the lab, I envisioned her smile. Beautiful, but also so strangely familiar. A part of me felt like I'd known her forever, and yet…

Surprised to find the door unlocked, I frowned. I'd given strict orders to everyone that all doors be kept locked at all times.

But as I pushed open the door, I realized that I wasn't the only one who'd come to work early. Charisma was already at her desk, her forehead in her hand as she struggled over an internal document.

"Good morning," I said, loud and intended to startle.

"Ah!" she let out as she jumped up from her chair. "Oh, darn you," she went on when she realized it was me.

Instantly, that bright smile lit up her face and her eyes danced with laughter.

"Orange," I said, looking at her.

"I beg your pardon?" she said with a tilt of her head.

I pointed to her dress. "Nice color. Vibrant. Uplifting."

Looking down at herself, she grabbed the skirt of the dress and swished it around her thighs. "I think so," she affirmed. "It's one of my favorite colors."

"It's not everyday that an employee beats me to the office," I said as I set a coffee in front of her then put the bag of bagels on the corner of her desk. "Did you sleep here?"

She blushed, her rosy cheeks highlighted her high cheekbones against her porcelain skin. Beautiful.

"No," she said as she sat back down. "But I think I actually worked during my sleep… you know, dreaming about all this."

She glanced at me from the corner of her eyes before looking away, blushing even furiously.

What else did she dreamed about I wondered?

"Was it fruitful?" I pulled up a chair and sat at the corner of her desk.

"A bit." She muttered, her eyes avoiding looking at mine. She looked at the bag. "What's that?"

"Bagels," I said as I took a sip of my coffee. "With cream cheese."

Her attempt to hide the pleased twinkle in her eyes failed. I could see that she was happy but didn't want to gush and make a big deal out of it.

Cute.

As I reached out to push the bag of bagels toward her, she reached out to take it. Our fingers touched and for a moment, I completely lost my breath. Electricity seared through me, and I was suddenly thankful to be sitting. My legs most certainly would have failed me, leaving me falling to my knees right there in front of her.

I stared at her for a prolonged moment before finally regaining a semblance of control. I released the bag and leaned back in my chair trying to understand what had happened.

Was I coming down with something? I remembered waking up in the last few days feeling like I needed a cold shower after some steamy dream. I couldn't remember what it was about, but I was definitely in need of some relief when I woke up.

Chinatown Christmas
(Chen Family Cuisine #1)

Damn. Get a grip, man.

"If I remember correctly," I said, trying my damnedest to sound normal. "You're working on your PhD, right?"

"That's right," she said.

"And yet, here you are bright and early ready to get my product launch ready on time."

She shrugged. "That's what you hired me for, right?"

"Well… ah… yes. Right. Um. Yeah… Absolutely." Damn, she had me stammering and looking for the right words to say. I usually never struggled to find the right words. "But Harold and Penny dropped the ball. Well… Penny did her best, but Harold really let me down. He should be the one here so early in the morning. You shouldn't have to make up for his incompetence."

Again she shrugged. There was something so pure and innocent in the way she took it all in. And there wasn't a trace of malice towards Harold, and damn if he didn't deserve it.

She reached out for the little container of cream cheese at the same time that I did. Once again, the light touch of her fingertips on my skin left me weak and hungry for more.

I gulped. Now I remembered my dream. It involved a lot of kissing…and touching with a certain woman. Charisma.

If she knew what I was thinking about right now, she would be blushing as red as a tomato.

Thank God she didn't read minds or else she'd think I was up to no good with her.

I watched as she spread cream cheese on her bagel.

Yeah, like I'd like to spread cream all over her and lick her up.

"Jake?" Charisma asked.

I snapped out of my thoughts and tried to focus on her words. Not at her mouth, her eyes, or her beauty.

Chinatown Christmas
(Chen Family Cuisine #1)

"Take me into your mouth," Charisma said.

My head jerked up. "What?" I asked.

"A piece of bagel right there on the corner of your mouth," Charisma said.

"Oh," I said, quickly wiping my mouth with a napkin.

"Give it to me hard," Charisma said.

"Um, what?" I asked.

Charisma blinked and said, "I admit, some of this can be hard. After all, we're missing a lot of data, and we're only days away from launch."

I turned around, adjusting my pants before turning back to face her.

"How can I help?" I asked.

"Bend me over like a bad bad boy," Charisma said.

"What did you say?" I asked.

"I said that Harold hiding some of the data like he did, has been a bad boy," Charisma shook her head. "He set us behind so much. But luckily," she smiled. "We still have time to make it work."

"Work, yes," I said. "Back to work. Focus on work. I need to focus on work."

Charisma nodded. "Yes, boss, nail me at work."

I blinked, and she was poring over some spreadsheet onscreen.

My mind was making things up, distracted from work for the first time in many years.

Never had a woman affected me so.

Chapter 7

<u>Charisma</u>

Jake Austin seemed a bit different from that day he brought me bagels and coffee in the morning. Ever since then, he seemed like a different person. Changed.

For one thing he came by my desk often, always asking how the project was going before heading off to wherever he was heading.

And when he would join my meetings with Penny and Harold, I would catch him glancing at me when he didn't think I was looking.

I still couldn't read his mind like I could with everyone else, especially Harold.

Now he really was an open book. Although he could be described as attractive in a skinny jeans, nerdy glasses and preppy kind of way, his thoughts were not attractive at all.

While he was smiling and friendly to the other co-workers at YouBite, I would catch his thoughts about them soon after his public display of affection.

Fake. Everything about him was so fake.

"Hello, ladies!" he announced as he came into the office with a box of donuts for the administrative staff. "I'd bought goodies for you beauties."

The three secretaries rushed over to the box, grabbing the donuts and inhaling them like air. "Thank you, Harold," they'd say. "You are such a gentleman."

"Delicious, Harold," one would say. "You always have such good taste."

You Hippos don't know good taste even if it bit you in your cottage cheese asses.

Harold's thought hit me like a slap in the face while he smiled happily at the secretaries. "Anything for my girls," he crooned.

"That's not a nice thing to say," I burst out.

The ladies looked at me and said, "What's not nice about Harold saying he'll do 'anything for my girls'?" Lizzie asked.

I realized I had spoken out loud about my own thought about Harold's inner thought. "He didn't mean it," I said.

"He gets us all kinds of nice things. Donuts today. The other day, he gave us all early Christmas gifts. Even Mr. Austin doesn't do that. He gives us the same thing every year on Christmas Day, a digital gift card to the local grocery store."

"Not that we're complaining about that," Stacy said. "But Harold is a lot more thoughtful."

You wouldn't think that of him if you knew what he thought of you all.

I bit my tongue. Who knew that being psychic or telepathic or whatever I am can be so troublesome.

"Hello, Charisma," Harold said, walking up to me and handing me a small box. "Here's your present."

"Thank you, Harold," I said. "I'm sorry I don't have a present for you today. I completely forgot."

Don't worry, Toots, I forgive you. While I don't think much about your ability to do your job, you're quite a sexy little thing, aren't you.

"What?" I asked, surprised at where Harold's thoughts had gone.

"That's okay, Charisma," Harold said, smiling. His eyes darted to my chest. "You don't need to give me a present."

Yeah, baby, I know how you can pay me back for that gift I gave you.

I opened the box and was surprised to find a dazzling diamond choker necklace.

"Wow, Harold," I gulped. "This is too much."

Harold came close to me to take it into his hands. He walked behind me and clasped the necklace around my neck.

I could feel the front of his groin press against my back and almost jumped. Harold was hard.

"I know how you can pay me back," he whispered into my ear, his breath hot against my skin.

I immediately saw what he was thinking. Me on my knees, servicing him.

I turned around to face him and almost slapped him when I heard a familiar voice.

"Beautiful!" Penny exclaimed, looking at the necklace Harold gave me.

"Of course it is," Harold said. "I wouldn't ever choose anything ugly, wouldn't I?"

It didn't take a psychic to know what he thought of Penny.

I took off the necklace and handed it to Penny. "I was just trying on the necklace, seeing how pretty it was, but it's really a gift from Harold to you," I told her.

Penny looked at Harold and squealed, giving him a huge hug.

Before I walked away, I whispered into Harold's ear.

"Perhaps you'd like Penny to pay you back the same way you wanted me to," I said.

Harold said, "It's just CZs. There's no way I want that thing near my little Harry."

"I should report you to HR, but unfortunately I need you to finish this Christmas project."

Harold looked down into my cleavage as a thought of his hit me.

Chinatown Christmas
(Chen Family Cuisine #1)

Maybe you can persuade me to actually work on this project if you'd give me some of that Afternoon Delight you're giving Jake every day.

Furious, I nearly punched Harold for his false accusation, all I did was walked off to my desk.

It was no secret to me that Harold had it out for me. But it was a well-hidden secret to the public and the rest of the staff at YouBite that Harold had this secret.

And only my psychic self knew it besides him.

Chapter 8

<u>Jake</u>

"Everyone's received their Christmas gifts, Mr. Austin," my HR manager/self-designated right hand person Cindy Marigold announced to me as she closed the doors to my office.

"Excellent," I said. "What did they say?"

Cindy shook her long red hair, "They were speechless at first, but then when they opened their envelopes, they all said, "Thank you, Mr. Austin."

I leaned back into my chair, crossed my arms above my head and said, "She did say it would be better if the staff received their presents before Christmas instead of on Christmas Day."

"Who?" Cindy asked.

I smiled. "Oh, Charisma."

Cindy frowned, "Oh her," she said. "The temp. Of course after Christmas holiday, she'll be gone soon enough."

"Why?" I asked, a sudden sense of panic came over me. Gone?

"We only have her for this holiday season, until Janet comes back after her maternity leave," Cindy said. "Charisma's only temporary. Like Christmas is. Here today. Gone tomorrow."

"Such talent, Cindy," I said sitting up. "Shouldn't be let go."

"Janet should be returning in January," Cindy said with a smile. "Then things get be back to the way it was."

"And you seem happy about that?" I asked her.

She walked over to me and placed her well-manicured hand on my elbow. "I followed you from your first start up to YouBite. You were always so focused, so direct."

"So I'm not now?"

"You seemed distracted. Not the kind of man who is driven to turn this startup into a bonafide company," Cindy said.

"I've been working non-stop for over five years to get this company to this stage. We'll make it this year, Cindy," I said.

"Not if you're distracted by the pretty face temp and all her sunshiny sunshine bursting out of the lab," Cindy said bitterly.

"You mean Charisma," I said, picturing her at her desk, poring over spreadsheets. "There's nothing wrong with her being so positive and peppy. The team needs that to get them motivated, especially around the holidays."

"There's just something about her…" Cindy said. She reached out to fix the collar of my shirt.

"Oh, today is the last day the staff is in before they take off for Christmas so you might want to make an appearance to see them off."

"Oh yes," I said. "Thanks for reminding me, Cindy."

Cindy smiled, her face closed to mine, "What would you do without me, Jake?"

"I don't know," I said, touching her cheek. Cindy had started as my personal secretary at my first start up years ago and had made her way to becoming head of my Human Resources. She was professional, no nonsense, and reliable.

She smiled as she looked into my eyes. "Janet'll be back. And if not, Harold can take over the department. He's got the degree and more years of experience than Ms. Chen."

"Harold?" I asked. Why did Cindy bring him up?

"Everyone likes Harold," Cindy said. "He's been here since the start of YouBite, Jake. I don' even know why you got Ms. Chen in. She hasn't done anything yet to move the project forward. Thanks to her, you're not going to hit your goal. You should just get rid of her."

"What?" I pulled away from her. "She's brought a lot to the table. We are moving forward. Why are you attacking Charisma?"

Cindy walked over to the door, opening it as she walked out. "The way you're acting, Jake. That passion, that emotional outburst. It's not you. And that's why you should get rid of Charisma Chen."

Cindy walked out as I took a deep breath to control my urge to call Cindy back into my office to fire her. That would have been my usual resort to any insubordination.

Cindy was wrong. Dead wrong.

But why did I feel that Charisma Chen had changed me forever?

Chapter 9

<u>Charisma</u>

"Did you see their faces?" I said to Jake as I watched the rest of the staff leave for the holidays. Now it was just down to the skeleton crew. Me, Harold, and Penny.

"Yeah, they seem happy," Jake said.

"That's because now you can get to see their faces when they receive their presents in person," I said.

Jake was about crack a smile when Cindy came by carrying her jacket and tote. "I still think giving them their gifts on Christmas is more appropriate," she said.

Jake was about to say something when Cindy reached up and kissed him on the lips. "I'm heading out," she said. "If you want some company on Christmas, you know where to find me."

Jake looked away.

I didn't know he and Cindy were together.

Cindy looked over at me. Her eyes burned with disdain and hate as she stared me down.

Take that, bitch. Jake Austin has and always will be mine. You're only temporary and will be gone soon enough.

Her thoughts hit me like a slap.

I looked over at Jake, but he had already walked away, leaving me with Cindy.

"So, you're in town for Christmas?" I asked.

"I stick around for when Jake needs me," she said. "After all, we go back. Way back. I know exactly what he needs."

"Really?" I asked, turning to look at her straight on. "He seems like he has a lot of things taken cared of. What does he need?"

Chinatown Christmas
(Chen Family Cuisine #1)

Cindy licked her lips. "Jake is closed off for a reason. He can't function if he gets distracted. That's how a genius works. Jake, he was a genius at setting up companies. Still is, but he's blocked. That's why it's taking him so long to get the business to this point, which to him, is way too long." Cindy sighed and looked me over. "But what does a graduate student like you with little experience know about starting and running a business."

"I have more business experience than you know," I said. "You've read my resume."

"What? Family business and then some internship at Procter and Gamble, then management trainee at some tech startup."

"I also rose from that trainee program to become manager and then director," I said. "Then we went public. Don't you remember reading that about me?"

"Well, excuse me," Cindy said. "I wasn't the one who hired you. Jake did. He requested resumes from your school, wanting to give a student a chance. Guess he was looking for a fresh perspective."

"Jake hired me himself?" I asked.

"He made that decision all on his own. Didn't even ask me for what I thought," Cindy said. "If it was me, I wouldn't have hired anyone. Harold could do Janet's job."

Her message was loud and clear. She didn't want me at YouBite.

"But Jake does," I said.

"Jake?" Cindy said, "he only hired you because there's too much work to do for Harold and Penny alone. And for your information, Jake and I...we're together. It's low-profile at work so nobody else knows. We like to keep it that way."

"I didn't know," I said.

Cindy's blue eyes cut through me. "So now you know."

She clearly didn't want me near Jake Austin.

"I might be off for a few days for the holidays, but I'm keeping my eyes on you. When this Christmas project fails, it will be all your fault."

She walked out of the lobby before I can say anything.

I stood there, stunned and angry at the same time. I felt like such a fool thinking Jake Austin was showing signs that he might be attracted to me. All that flirting and being nice to me…it was only a game to him. He was with someone else, and yet he was making those eyes at me. Those golden beautiful eyes of desire at me.

That jerk!

Chapter 10

<u>Jake</u>

"Jake," Mom said on the phone. "You can still fly out to spend Christmas with us."

"I can't, Mom," I said. "We are way behind. There is no way I can leave my team to sort this mess we're in now."

"I thought you've found someone who can take charge of your Christmas project," Mom said.

"She's good and very hard-working, but one person, especially someone new, can't just step in and fix the mess we're in. Charisma is smart and have good ideas, but she's still trying to get her head wrap around our project. Plus it's not her responsibility."

"Charisma, huh," Mom said. "I like her name. Is she as charismatic as her name?"

"Mom," I said firmly, "we're strictly co-workers. But since you asked, she is very much like her name. Charismatic, full of life, vibrant. I'm hoping she can breathe some fresh air into our company. That's why I hired her."

"Well, she sounds like the right person for the job. Just trust her and she'll come through."

"I wished I could, Mom," I said.

"What is she…fresh out of college? Twenty-one? Just a babe?" Mom asked.

"No, she's a PhD student at USC, has a stellar work experience, is very capable, has leadership abilities and strong sensibility…"

"Oh, she sounds wonderful. Are you dating her, son?" Mom asked.

I thought about Charisma's lips which were soft, plump, and so kissable.

"Don't tell me, a girl like that's probably already engaged or married. And to someone handsome, successful, and upstanding."

"Nope," I said. "I'm not dating her. As far as her being single… I haven't even asked or noticed. Been too busy with the project."

"Jake," Mom said. "It's okay to take some time out of work in order to have a life, to meet someone special and form a relationship with them."

I knew what Mom was getting at, and why she was saying what she was saying in that particular way.

When I was younger, I was diagnosed as being on the Spectrum. Everything had to be a certain way. I had to be super focused on tasks and on goals in order to get things done.

My super focus kept me on my goals, and made me a success in school and business. But when it came to my social life, that was something else.

Mom was reminding me to have a social life. Even to meet a woman so I can have a relationship.

"Mom, I know you're only asking because you care about me, but I do have relationships with women, remembered I told you at Thanksgiving."

"Well, name one whom you've seen more than once," Mom said.

I thought about all the models, actresses, and pretty arm candy types I've dated. Not seriously though.

"There," Mom said. "You couldn't even name one."

I then thought of Cindy, who had been a casual fling off and on throughout the years. When I started my first company out of my college dorm room, Cindy was a classmate who joined me in my first venture, along with two other guys.

She was also someone I hooked up with now and then in college. We weren't in a relationship, but we did see each other once in a while throughout the years.

"Cindy," I said. "That's a woman whom I've seen a few times. She also works at YouBite."

"Well then," Mom said, almost giddy. "That's a start. You can bring Cindy back home to meet us for Christmas. That'll be perfect."

"Mom…"

"See you for Christmas," Mom said.

Before I can say, "I can't," Mom had hung up.

"Great, just great," I said. "Mom is expecting me and Cindy for Christmas."

A knock on the door startled me.

I thought everyone had left for the day.

But of course, Charisma, the hardest worker since I hired her, was peeking inside my office. The door was open because I thought everyone had left.

Was she standing there all this time I was on the phone with my mother?

"Jake," Charisma said. "I need you to see something."

"Just a sec," I said, pointing my finger up as though it is beckoning her to wait. I texted my mother that I can't make it back home for Christmas so please don't make plans.

When I was done, I turned to Charisma.

"What is it that you wanted me to see?"

Her face was no longer smiling, and she seemed to be glaring at me.

Was it something that I did wrong?

I followed her to the lab and to her desk. On her desk was a box.

The present I gave her for Christmas. I smiled. I remembered going downtown to pick it out for her, thinking it would match her jade green lace dress she wore the other day.

"What's the meaning of this?" she asked, pointing to the gold and green jade dropped earrings that I had bought from a local jewelry store. They were delicate, regal-looking, and elegant.

"You don't like them?" I asked her. "Genuine jade and gold. I saw them the other day and thought they would look nice with your green dress."

She was livid. "That would sound so sweet coming from someone else, but from you, it sounds…" She quickly boxed up the earrings and handed it to me. "Keep it. I can't take it. It's inappropriate of you giving me a gift like this."

"Is it appropriate for Harold to give you a diamond-encrusted necklace?" I asked.

"You saw the gift he gave me?" Charisma asked.

"I saw him put that necklace on you," I said, remembering how I didn't like that Harold had his grubby hands on her. The idea of another man touching Charisma made my blood boil.

"That's an inappropriate gift too," Charisma said, crossing her arms.

"So you don't like receiving jewelry as gifts?" I asked.

"No," Charisma shook her head, "I love jewelry, especially as gifts, but not when it's meant for something. A girl's not supposed to accept something like that if it means something else."

"I've given jewelry to lots of girls," I said.

Charisma's eyes widen. "I knew you were popular, but not that popular!"

"It's just jewelry," I said.

"I know you're worth billions, right?" Charisma said. "This little trinket probably means nothing to you, but to a girl like me, it means selling yourself out. If you know nothing about me, know that I won't do it."

She was angry, she looked like she wanted to slap me, throw something at me.

"Hey, hey," I threw my hands up in the air. "Whatever." I took the box of earrings with me and walked out of the lab.

What had gotten into Charisma just now?

I don't know what happened, but it'll just be business as usual with her. Strictly professional and nothing else.

Chapter 11

<u>Sally</u>

"Sally!" Mom called out from the dining room where she was clearing a table. "Where's your sister?"

"How am I supposed to know," I said. But I understood her concern.

Charisma hadn't come to the restaurant the last four nights and Mom and Dad were growing worried about her.

They hid it well, or at least they thought they did. Mom discretely asked questions about what

129

Charisma had eaten while Dad was more concerned with how much sleep she was getting.

"What are you making?" Dad said as he came up behind me.

I smiled. Having taken the initiative to find a suitable recipe, I'd come upon one that was perfect for the situation.

"Clarity Chive Ginger Dumplings," I said.

His smile told of the pride he felt at that very moment. "You're getting the hang of this a lot quicker than I expected. Clarity Dumplings… I assume for Charisma."

I nodded.

"Good work, Sally. Very intuitive of you."

"Thanks, Dad."

But as I prepared to move on to the next step in my Clarity dish, I came upon a special ingredient. I looked around the kitchen, went to the few potted herbs that were on the shelf, looked in the spice rack and then went back in the storeroom.

Chinatown Christmas
(Chen Family Cuisine #1)

"What in heavens are you looking for?" Mom said as she set a stack of dishes on the counter.

"Chives," I said.

"Out," Mom said. "We're out. You'll have to go back home to our private garden. I know that we have three thriving plants out by the basil."

"Home," I said, hearing the childish whine in my voice. "I don't have time to go back home."

Dad, busily working on the dough for the dumplings looked at me from under his brow.

I knew what it meant. It meant, listen to your mother.

Ripping off my apron, I plopped it on the counter and headed out the back door.

When I reached the home that I still shared with my parents, I didn't bother going inside, but went around to the backyard, a large portion of which was devoted to the garden. I found the three tall tufts of chives.

One had already begun to pop out deep purple blooms… and that was the chive that I needed for this special recipe.

I snipped precisely what I needed and not a blade more and dropped it in a small paper bag.

Hurrying back to the restaurant, I thought of Charisma and everything she was going through. While I knew that, as my older sister, she was more than capable of taking care of herself, I couldn't help but wonder what was really going on with her.

"These dumplings aren't going to fill themselves," Dad called out when I returned to the kitchen.

"I've got the chives," I said.

"Get to it."

I worked on the special filling, added the chives that I'd chopped up, then made a special dipping sauce that also had a sprinkling of chives on top.

"Thank you, Clay," Mom said, coming up beside Dad.

He looked at her, his love for her apparent in his eyes. "What for, Dazzle?"

She leaned her head on his arm. "For working on this for Charisma. You know how worried I am about her. All of this working day and night… it's going to wear her out and she's not going to know what hit her."

Dad smiled. "You'll see," he said, reassuring her. "This special dish is so nutritious, it will give Charisma all the energy she needs, and then some."

As they went on, exchanging their concerns for Charisma, I poured the dipping sauce into a small container and snapped on the cover, then put a dozen dumplings into a larger container and sealed it tight.

"Well, Charisma's dinner is ready," I said.

"Benji is already out on a delivery," Mom said.

"That's okay," I said. "I'll go. I'm curious to see this gorgeous place where Charisma works."

I put the dinner in a paper bag and headed out, arriving at YouBite well past closing time.

When I reached the front door, I pushed into it but found it was locked. I knocked to try to get the attention of the guard inside. Concentrating on his phone and with earphones tucked in deep, he was oblivious to my presence.

I pulled out my phone and texted Charisma.

Hey, big shot. Your little sister is standing in the cold with your hot dumplings. Think you could take a minute to come open up? The guard is ignoring me.

Seconds later, she responded.

On my way.

Moments later, she stepped out of the elevator. With long, elegant strides, she walked through the lobby of the mega company as if she owned it.

Chinatown Christmas
(Chen Family Cuisine #1)

She was confident, but not cocky. Charisma didn't have an arrogant bone in her body, and it made me marvel all the more. Always so chipper. Always so positive. Sometimes I wondered how she did it.

"Sorry to make you wait," she said as she opened the door. She took a whiff of the evening air. "It's not cold out here," she added with an amused chuckle as she gestured for me to come in.

"Just wanted to make you feel a little guilty," I said with a teasing grin.

"It worked," she said. "I dropped everything and literally ran down the hall to the elevator."

"Wow," I gushed as I looked around. "What a cool place to work in. It's so massive. How high does that ceiling go?"

She joined me in looking up.

"Too high," she said with a laugh.

Handing her the paper bag, I held her gaze.

"What is it?" she said.

"I'm happy for you."

She smiled, and even blushed slightly.

"You seem so happy," I went on. "Happier than I've ever seen you. Yet you're working all the time. How…?" I bit my lip and looked around, trying to understand. "How can you be happy working all the time?"

"This is what I've always dreamed of, Sally," she said. "Maybe I didn't envision working at such a large company, but the work that I do… I really love it. It's what I've been studying for all these years."

Nodding, I smiled. "Okay. I get it."

"Not to mention the excitement of taking part in the development of a new product. It's thrilling… more than I would have thought."

Out from the same elevator Charisma had emerged from came a very handsome and tall man, his dark hair tousled and falling over his hazel or was it golden eyes after a long day at work.

"Who is that?" I whispered.

Charisma glanced back as the tall man came our way. "Oh, that's my boss, Jake Austin."

I couldn't help but smile. "Oh, Char. Now I really understand. No wonder you enjoy working late. I would too if I had to look into those dreamy eyes."

The closer he got, the better he looked. He was like a hero pulled straight out of a hot and steamy romance novel. I'd read of his type too many times. The smoldering eyes. The kissable lips. The strong hands.

Oh, damn, girl, I wanted to say.

"Everything okay here?" he said as he reached us. His tone was a lot harsher than his appearance let on. While he appeared friendly and approachable, his tone was anything but. "I got a notification upstairs that the front door had opened."

"Just my sister dropping off some dumplings for dinner."

He looked at me. His lips smiled slightly; a smile that never reached his eyes.

"Okay," he said. "Don't forget to lock up after she leaves." Saying nothing more, he turned and left us.

"Cold," I said.

"He has his moments," Char said.

"But, girl… you two sure do look hot together. You're a perfect fit for each other."

"Ha!" she let out. "That's ridiculous."

I turned to head out. "Anyway, wait until I tell Mom and Dad why you're spending so much time at…" I brought my hands up for air quotes. "…the office. It's not for the work. It's for the really cute boss."

She glanced back at her boss who had yet to board the elevator. "He might be easy on the eyes, but… believe me, that cold front isn't just for late night intruders. He is a real grump."

"Well, maybe feeding him some of our world-famous awesome food would change that," I said. "After all, having Chen's Family Cuisine is magical," I said.

Charisma said, "Did someone make a dish in here called, "Stay away Spicy Duck? Because at this moment, that's what I want."

Charisma's eyes teared up but she quickly wiped it away.

"What's wrong?" I asked.

"The project's not going as well as I liked. I keep running into obstacles. And Jake…he was nice for a while, but now I know why. It's awful because I really liked him, too."

"Oh Char," I hugged her. "I'm so sorry you're going through all of this. Can you quit?"

Char pulled away and shook her head. "I won't quit, Sally. I can't. I'm not a quitter. Just because some things are a challenge doesn't mean I should quit. I want to turn things around. I believe I can turn things around. But I just need some time."

Her eyes were determined, and she was clenching her hands into fists. Char had never quit on anything before. She wasn't going to now.

"Good," I said, encouraging her. "If there's anyone who can turn things around, it's you, Char. You can make it happen."

Chapter 12

<u>Charisma</u>

Christmas was right around the corner, and the way things were going, it was not going to be merry.

"Three days," Jake said as he came to my desk. "You have three days left to get this thing ready."

"I know, Mr. Austin," I said.

Turning on his heel he left the lab just as abruptly as he'd arrived. Tension grew everyday and the entire team felt it.

As I had everyday for the past week, I went to Harold. "Where are we with the vendors?"

He didn't even have the guts to look up at me. "Some of them dropped out."

"What?" I said, not sure I'd heard him right. "And please look at me when I'm speaking to you."

With a sour taste in his mouth, he looked up at me. "Several vendors have had to drop out of the program."

"Why?"

"Short supply."

"Come again?"

"There's a short supply of goods."

Penny came to my side. "That's not all. The marketing team that was hired to take care of the campaign let us down. Their designer apparently got sick. They weren't able to get the sample design completed."

"Did I hear right?" a booming voice called out.

Chinatown Christmas
(Chen Family Cuisine #1)

We all turned to Jake as he stormed back into the lab.

"Did I just hear that right?" he barked, clearly in a panic. "We lost vendors because of a supply chain shortage? And what happened to our marketing?"

"You guys get back to work," I ordered Penny and Harold. "Come on, Mr. Austin."

I led him to my desk and sat him down.

"Breathe, Mr. Austin. Breathe."

"I am breathing," he shot back as he rubbed his temple between his index finger and thumb.

"You're panting," I said with a teasing grin. "And it's not a good look on you."

At this, he stopped breathing altogether and looked up at me with a blank stare. Then he suddenly burst out laughing.

"Holy shit," he said through his on-going chuckle. Shaking his head, he looked at me with a sheepish grin. "You sure have a way with me, don't you?"

I nodded. If I had to be on friendly terms with Jake to get this project done, I would. Since that day I rejected his earrings, which I hoped sent a clear message to him to keep our relationship friendly but professional, he had acted just that.

"And it's a good thing that I do," I said as I sat behind my desk. "Now that you've broken through this little panic attack, let's attack this launch."

"The way things are looking, there's not going to be a launch."

"There will be a launch," I said. "And it will be a huge success." I pulled a folder out from the pile on my desk. "You heard Harold announce this sudden pull back from some of the vendors. The ones who dropped out couldn't get their ingredients. They're in short supply. So…" I opened my folder. "A while back… just in case… I've started looking into other possibilities… alternative. Local farms may be able to get us out of this tight spot. And some vendors even grow their own ingredients."

Jake cocked his brow. "Local farms?"

I pulled out a list of small, sometimes artisanal farms and showed it to him. "The first dozen or so can easily supply dairy products. The next group can supply small amounts of grains and nuts. And finally, fresh produce. The only thing we're missing now is where to get our beef and poultry."

He looked at me, nodding.

"How much sleep did you get last night?" I suddenly said as I noticed the dark circles under his eyes.

He shrugged.

"Clearly not enough, right?"

He shrugged again.

"Look," I said as I stood. "I've held onto these as backups for a while. But with what Harold just announced, I'm not going to take any chances. I'll split this list between the three of us and we'll figure this out. We'll find the suppliers that we need."

He looked up at me, a tired smile on his pale face.

"Get some rest, Mr. Austin," I said as I patted his shoulder. "You don't want to look like a ghost of yourself the night of the launch."

*****

With suppliers signed up and committed, we were closer to a successful launch than ever. My heart was pumping, my adrenaline was going, and the urgent rhythm at the office was like a good song that just kept me going and going.

The excitement grew the closer to completion we got.

"Damn it!" Jake said as he stormed in. "Where are we on this project?"

We all turned to him, stunned by the explosive entrance.

"The product is ready to go, Mr. Austin. We're ready to go."

"Are you?" he spat back.

I stood up, my fists on my hips, ready to face off with him. "If you have any criticism of my work, stop beating around the bush and make your criticism clear."

"What happened to the design work?" he said, holding my gaze.

I turned to Penny who'd been tasked with clearing that up.

Pressing her lips into an apologetic line, she shrugged.

"Great," Jake let out as his hands rose to his sides and fell back down, slapping his thighs. "That's just great. Just great!"

"I think I might know somebody who can help us," I said.

"It's a little late for that now, Charisma," Jake said.

"She works fast… and… she owes me one," I added with a playful grin.

He calmed down and was finally ready to listen to me.

"My sister, Tammy," I said. "Not only is she artistic, but she is very social media savvy. She has a large and very loyal following. I guess you could call her an influencer."

Jake stared blankly at me.

"She'll be able to get the word out," I said. "Trust me."

Chapter 13

Christmas day was coming fast and there was still far too much to do.

As expected, Tammy came through, getting us great graphics and more marketing materials than we could ever use.

"I have to hand it to you, Charisma," Penny said after I'd shown her the short video Tammy had produced. "That is a great video. She built up interest and intrigue about the product. She hinted just enough without giving too much away."

"Think Mr. Austin will like it?" I said.

"I don't see why he wouldn't." She looked at me, suddenly shy and hesitant.

"What is it?" I said. "Is there something I'm missing?"

"A name."

"Huh?"

"A good product name," Penny said. "We'd temporarily named it The 2022 Good Dish, but we never came up with an official and more enticing name we're announcing on Christmas Day."

"That's right." My gaze darted around my desk, looking for my next move. "Okay," I finally said as I got up and headed for the door. "I'll be back in an hour."

I left the office and headed to the Chen Family Cuisine Restaurant. We needed to brainstorm and find something suitable to call this new product.

"Is Tammy here?" I shouted as I walked in.

Noticing a few patrons in the dining room, I offered them an apologetic shrug and went back into the kitchen.

Chinatown Christmas
(Chen Family Cuisine #1)

And there she was, preparing dishes for the diners.

"Oh," she said on seeing me, her eyes instantly filling with concern. "Is there something wrong with the videos I gave you? Did your boss not like them?"

I went to her and gave her a big hug. "You're amazing, Tammy. And you're a life saver." I looked around the kitchen. "I can't believe that you managed to get so much work done and you're still here cooking at the restaurant on top of it all."

She laughed. "Char, social media is my thing. As much as I love working here with Mom and Dad, all that social media stuff is my fun stuff. That's me playing. That's me having a good time. In fact, I've completed all I need for social media. Just this morning I put something up on TikTok, and you should see the response I got. People want to know about YouBite."

I smiled. "You're a genius."

Her hands on her hips, she looked at me. "Then what are you doing here?"

"I need a name," I said.

"Who's name?"

"A product name. I've just been informed, barely forty-eight hours before the soft launch, that this product does not have an official name."

Tammy glanced over at Mom who was at the sink rinsing out a pot.

"What's going on?" I said, looking from one to the other

"Funny," Tammy said. "But ever since I started working on this thing, I've been calling it… wait for it…"

She was killing me.

"The Dazzler Delight," she said with a beaming grin.

Gaping, I stared at them. "That's insane."

Chinatown Christmas
(Chen Family Cuisine #1)

Mom came to me, a slightly hurt expression on her face. "I thought it was kind of funny putting my name on it. You don't like it?"

I grasped her shoulders. "Like it? I love it. It's insanely genius. The Dazzler Delight. It's perfect. I love you guys. I've got to get back to work."

Skipping and hopping all the way, I went back to the office. I bounded out of the elevator and headed straight for Jake's office. Neglecting to knock, I opened the doors and announced, "The Dazzler Delight."

He looked up from his desk, a frown of his face. "What the hell are you doing barging in…"

"The Dazzler Delight will be launching Christmas day," I said, my smile so wide, I thought it would crack my face in two.

He stared at me. The frown left his brow and he slowly stood up. It was sinking in. The name that we'd found for the product was sinking in. His eyes softened and his lips curled up into a faint smile.

"The Dazzler Delight," he said softly to himself.

"That's right." I held my breath, waiting for him to officially give his okay.

He came around to the front of his desk and leaned back on it.

"Sir," I said. "Do we go forward with the name? We need to inform the packaging department."

A full-blown smile lit up his face. I'd never seen him look so happy, so relieved... so beautiful. He nodded. "Give the go ahead."

Thrilled, I clapped and hopped as I turned around and headed for the door.

"Charisma," he called out as I opened the door. "Where d'you get the idea?"

"I'm sad to say that I have no merit in this. It's my sister, Tammy. She's been calling it the

Dazzler Delight ever since she started working on the project.”

“I’m going to have to meet this sister of yours.”

“One more thing I need to tell you about the name,” I said, unsure how he would respond. “The name refers to my mother, Dazzle.”

Nodding like a bobblehead, he came to me. “That’s one hell of a family you’ve got there.”

“I can’t argue with that,” I said, suddenly growing solemn. “My sisters are the best siblings anyone could hope for, and my parents worked hard and brought us up right.”

“I can see that.” He pressed a tight smile. “If things continue this way, I may just have to hire your entire family.”

I laughed and fully opened the door. “They might be a little too busy for that. After all, they do have a family restaurant to run.” I glanced back at him as I walked away. "But I'll ask them. Would be fun to have them here at YouBite."

He followed me out into the hall. "Wait a minute. What did you say?"

"It'd be fun."

"No, before that."

"They're too busy?"

"Busy with what?"

"The family restaurant."

"You never told me your family ran a restaurant."

I chuckled. "You never asked."

"Charisma," he said in all seriousness as he stopped me and turned to face me. "I think that your family's restaurant should be added to our list of vendors. They'd be a great partner to YouBite."

Tilting my head to the side, I looked up at him. The idea had never even crossed my mind. "Really?"

"Sure," he went on. "YouBite is an online app that connects eaters with restaurants and grocery stores. And with our special Christmas product this year… it's a perfect fit. The Dazzler Delight; a special gift box of exquisite gold delicacies. What could be better than that?"

I smiled, pleased with his suggestion. "I'll be sure to talk to them about it. A partnership between YouBite and Chen Restaurant could be very interesting. I just fear that there might be a conflict of interest."

"Not on my end," he said. "Talk to them."

He left me and returned to his office, while I pulled out my phone to call my dad.

"What's up, Char?" he said.

"I have an interesting proposition for you."

"I'm all ears."

"How about partnering with YouBite. Chen Restaurant would be a supplier/vendor."

He was silent for a moment. "You trust this YouBite guy? Is he on the up and up?"

I nodded and smiled as I held the phone to my ear. "I think it could be very good for everyone involved."

"I trust your judgement, Char. Sign us up."

At the lab, I sat at my desk for all of five minutes as I prepared the paperwork that would unite my family's enterprise with YouBite.

With the contract in hand, I headed back to Jake's office to finalize his part of the deal.

"Are you ready to sign on the dotted line?" I said as I entered his office. The move was becoming more and more familiar and easy.

"They're on board?" he said as he signed the contract.

"On board and eager to get started," I said as I held onto the document while he signed. "All that remains is getting my dad's signature and we're ready to go."

*****

Chinatown Christmas
(Chen Family Cuisine #1)

After work, I sat in the restaurant's dining room with my dad as he carefully read every line of the contract. The restaurant was closed for the day, and we had the whole place to ourselves.

"Feels strange," he said.

"What feels strange, Dad?"

"We've never advertised before."

Shocked, I sat back and looked at him. "Never?"

"Never. No ads. No promotions. Nothing."

Considering the number of people that sat in that very dining room every night, it was hard to believe that we'd never advertised before.

"In fact, this is the first time that this restaurant and the recipes from our family cookbook have found such popularity. To find this degree of appreciation for our family recipes, you have to go back to the 1920s in China."

Setting my elbows on the table, I leaned into my hands and listened intently to him.

"Your great, grand aunt, used one of these recipes to fake her own death in order to escape prison."

"Dad! Really?" I said, instantly perked up. "You never told me that story before."

He looked at me with a solemn smile. "It's a story of great bravery and strength."

"I have no doubt. Please, tell me how she got out."

"A wise young woman, she learned and memorized these ancient recipes. By the time she was wedded at only seventeen, she knew all the recipes by heart. Unfortunately, she wasn't able to use that knowledge because her new husband was a wealthy man who had servants and cooks who took care of everything."

He played with the corner of the contract, going back in time as he went on with the story.

Chinatown Christmas
(Chen Family Cuisine #1)

"During the Cultural Revolution, they were thrown out of their house."

"Their own house?"

Dad nodded. "As if that wasn't bad enough, her husband abandoned her, left her behind when he was trying to escape the new regime."

Woe. And I thought I had it rough sometimes. That certainly put my little problems into perspective.

"She was captured by revolutionaries and put in prison. She hadn't been there long when she began to show signs of losing her mind. Someone in the prison, it is not known who… they took pity on her and agreed to cook one of her special soups from the recipes she'd learned and memorized. After eating the soup which had the capacity to reduce one's heartrate to near zero, guards at the prison thought she was dead."

I smiled. "That's genius."

"But her journey wasn't over," Dad said. "Her 'body' was unceremoniously thrown into a ditch along with dozens of dead prisoners. She had to stay there, motionless until the sun went down. The bodies of two emaciated men were thrown over her, and she had to just lie there beneath them."

"Oh my," I muttered, biting the tips of my fingers.

"In the dark, she finally crawled out of the ditch and escaped. She came to the United States and started a whole new life, but she never forgot where she came from."

"That's amazing, Dad. What an amazing life. What an amazing woman."

Dad nodded. "She did, indeed, have an amazing life. If you want to know more, I'd invite you to watch the film The Last Emperor."

Frowning, I looked at him. "Huh?"

"The movie shows what happened to her. You see, she was the last Empress of China."

"My great, grand aunt was an empress?"

Chinatown Christmas
(Chen Family Cuisine #1)

Smiling, he nodded. "Empress Elizabeth… or Wanrong. And, in the movie, she was played by Joan Chen."

"I don't believe it," I muttered. "An empress… And the very last empress of China. Wow."

We sat in silence for a long while as I fully digested this new information.

"I understand now," I said softly, reverently. "I understand the importance of all these family recipes. Our ancestors really did amazing things, and it is all worthy of guarding, protecting and, of course, passing it down to future generations."

Dad grasped my hand and squeezed as he smiled at me, a tear glistening in the corner of his eye.

Chapter 14

<u>Jake</u>

The day to get everything ready to go had finally arrived. The last twenty-four hours. As I waited with Charisma and Penny, hundreds of people around the world were waiting by the phone, ready to take orders as of midnight.

Countries abroad, working in their own time zone, would be taking orders shortly.

Sitting across from Charisma, I was hopeful. We'd make this happen.

"Mr. Austin," Penny said as she hung up the phone and came to us.

I turned to her, not sure I wanted to hear what she had to say.

Chinatown Christmas
(Chen Family Cuisine #1)

"It's not good," she said. "I'm so sorry to have to be the one to tell you, Mr. Austin, but…"

I shrugged and bit my lip, steeling myself for more bad news.

"The warehouse and shipping facility are empty."

"That can't be," I argued.

"I'm sorry. Apparently the shipment of Dazzler Delight was not delivered… well, that is… they were not delivered to the proper facility. They were delivered to a facility in Connecticut… and in different packages…"

I groaned.

"And… they're not assembled."

It was a cascade of bad news that seemed endless. "Is that all?" I muttered.

Charisma glanced at me with concern as I buried my face in my hands, ready to cry out in aggravation.

"Shit," I let out. It would take at least a week to find the five to ten people needed… people who could work full time to assemble the product.

"How could this happen?" I muttered, looking at Charisma and Penny. "How did things go so wrong?"

"Let me go check on a few things," Charisma said as she turned to her computer.

I got up and went to look over her shoulder, eager to catch anything that she might miss.

"What's going on?" she said as she tried to gain access to her documents. She entered her password again and again.

Nothing.

"Let me try." I tapped in my own password, bypassing her security clearance. "There."

She pulled up the necessary documents. "Wait a minute," she said, reading her screen. "This isn't right. This isn't what I… Damn."

"Hacked?"

Chinatown Christmas
(Chen Family Cuisine #1)

She looked up at me. "I think so." She pointed to her screen. "Look at this. The logistics have been changed. Delivery addresses have been altered. Delivery instructions have also been tampered with and… Oh no. And look at this. Someone changed 'assembled' for 'unassembled'. I don't get it. Who could do such a thing… and why?"

"Look through your history," I suggested.

She checked the log. "No," she muttered softly. "How could he?"

I looked over her shoulder.

Harold.

"How could he do this. He came in here and deliberately sabotaged your launch," she said looking up at me with the most forlorn look in her eyes. "Why would he do this? He rewrote every single instruction I'd written."

"I think I might have an idea," I said as I walked away.

She quickly got up and followed me as I left the lab and headed to my office. Without waiting to be invited in, she walked right in and up to my desk.

"There," I said as I picked up an envelope that had been left on my desk. "I had noticed it this morning but was so preoccupied with everything else that I put it aside."

"Do you think it's from Harold?" Charisma said.

I opened it and read:

Nice work Jake. I've been with YouBite for over three years and this is how you choose to treat me? You know damn well that I should have been the one to be in charge of this project when Janet took her maternity leave. Instead, you decided to hire some fucking Miss Sunshine all Day.

Well, let's see if your darling Charisma can work her way out of this one.

Chinatown Christmas
(Chen Family Cuisine #1)

Good luck, asshole. I quit.

"So that's why he was so cold towards me… right from the start," Charisma said. "He thinks that I stole his place."

I shook my head, holding back my anger at Harold. I'll deal with him later, but now, we have a real problem at hand.

"I should have anticipated this," I said, "But…"

"It's not your fault, Jake. Just leave it to me," she said. "I'll fix this."

"How?"

"Trust me. As soon as the orders start coming in, I'll make sure the deliveries go out."

It was my turn to follow her as we returned to the lab. No sooner had her butt hit her chair that she was on the phone with the warehouse in Connecticut, putting together an assembly team.

Then she got on her computer. "Here's what I'll do," she said as she busily typed on her keyboard. "Instead of placing a direct order for the product, we'll sell them a subscription instead."

"A subscription?" I said, not following her logic.

"Yeah," she said with her ever optimistic smile. "We'll offer a special promotion. Something like – buy a gift card and get a two-month supply of special delight for free. We'll inform them that their first order will arrive one week after Christmas."

I looked at her. I wanted to yank her out of her chair and pull her into my arms and thank her for not only saving the launch, but potentially saving the reputation of YouBite.

"You're a genius," I said softly, simply amazed at how quickly she'd found a solution.

She held up her hands and crossed her fingers. "Let's just hope it works."

"Good work," I said. "Really good work. Let's get that sent out and get some rest. You deserve it."

Chapter 15

<u>Charisma</u>

After some scrambling and then finally leaving the office late, I went home and slept fitfully for a full five hours, the most I've slept in weeks. I was dead tire, but excited at the same time. YouBite's product was going to launch, and I was a part of that launch.

When it was five o'clock in the morning, I was already up and ready to go to the office. I couldn't wait to see how the launch went.

"Bet you never thought you'd be spending Christmas day with your boss," Jake said looking over my comfy red Christmas sweater, leggings, and warm fuzzy boots. Jake had beat me to the office. And unlike me, he was dressed impeccably in a dark cashmere sweater and jeans.

"It's Christmas Day," I said. "I always dress cozy and comfy on Christmas morning."

Jake smiled and said, "Of course. Who wouldn't." He handed me a cup of coffee and a small bag. Bagels.

I had to smile. "Thank you," I said. I'd learned to accept small gestures of gratitude from Jake, the grump. It was rare, but when it came, it was amusing.

"Well, it's Christmas. I do have a heart underneath all this grumpiness, you know," Jake said wryly.

"I never said you were a Scrooge," I muttered, not looking at Jake.

"You don't have to," Jake said. "I know what my reputation is at YouBite. Look, I have a few things to take care of," Jake said, heading to his office. "Then we'll see how all of our hard work these last few days had paid off."

"Sure," I said, heading to my desk in the lab. I had come to see this area as a second home, having spent more time here than my own in the last few days. When Janet returns from maternity leave in January, I would miss this place.

I would go back to being a full-time graduate student and spend my entire time writing my thesis before graduating with a doctorate. After that, my path as a PhD would probably include consulting, research and or teaching at an university.

"So how did our launch go?" a familiar female voice cheerfully announced.

Penny.

"We're still giving it some time. You know. People get up, open their presents, and then after that, if they had gift cards or anything like that, they end up buying things later in the day," I said.

Penny had deep bags under her eyes, her hair was not combed, and she kept yawning. Poor Penny!

"Okay," she sat down into her desk chair and wiped her eyes. "I'll wait with you to see."

I went over to Penny and said, "It'll take a few hours. You've done all you can at this point. Why don't you go home and get some sleep. I'm sure your family would love to see you on Christmas."

"But don't you need me here?" Penny asked.

"Penny, you've been so hard-working and helpful, but at this stage, there was little you could do."

"What about order-taking?" Penny asked. "That would require all hands on deck, wouldn't it?"

"Don't worry, Penny," I said. "We've got that covered."

She didn't know I had sent the rest of the staff home, leaving me alone with Jake to salvage what we could of the launch. I had convinced Jake to give the rest of the staff Christmas day off since we would be able to handle the orders ourselves because of the programming I had come up with to take the orders automatically.

We were no longer relying on live order-taking but on a seamless online sales process. People were used to this, and YouBite was a tech company so should be completely streamlined.

My doctorate thesis was on the process of digitalization. YouBite served as the perfect company for me to see how it would work.

But first, we had to transition the past customers of YouBite, used to the hands-on order-taking and customer service.

That's what Jake and I was on hand for, but also to give our launch a personal touch. You can talk to the CEO and to the Head Product Manager, which was Jake and me, on Christmas Day to place your orders.

So much of the day was spent on the phone, giving orders, verifying orders and giving out even more orders. By the time seven o'clock rolled around, I was ready to give up. We'd done the best we could.

"Thanks for all your help," Jake said as he hung up the phone and sat back in his chair. "It might not be the launch I'd hoped for, but at least it's not the catastrophe that Harold tried to turn it into."

"Right. Well, I'm glad I could help."

He stood and wiped his palms on his slacks, essentially ironing out some invisible wrinkle. "I'm going to grab some dinner. There's this little Chinese restaurant down the road from here."

"Is that so?" I said with a cunning grin.

"Yeah," he went on. "The food is great, and the atmosphere is quietly festive."

"Quietly festive. That's an interesting description."

"Want to join me?" he said.

Taken aback, I leaned into my chair and looked up at him. Never had he come to the restaurant with anyone.

"What about Cindy?" I blurted. It had been on the back of my mind the last few days as I worked side-by-side with Jake. Didn't he spend any time with his girlfriend instead of at the office? Especially on Christmas?

Jake looked confused. "Cindy? Why would I invite her?"

"I thought…"

Jake's eyes widen with understanding, and he drew a deep breath before letting it out. "So that was what the whole earrings incident was about. You thought Cindy was my girlfriend?"

I nodded.

Jake turned to face me as he took my hands. "I need to tell you something."

I waited to hear him out.

"Cindy. She's no longer with YouBite. I had to let her go."

I couldn't help letting my mouth drop open.

"Last night after you left, I did some digging into the project's origin, and found that Cindy had helped Harold sabotage the project from the start. She had promised him the top position in the department, if he sabotages the project."

"He did, but it doesn't make sense for her to want to ruin your project," I said.

"I thought so, too, especially since she wanted to see YouBite go public soon after the project is launched and is a success," Jake said.

"So she was trying to sabotage YouBite from going public," I said.

"Yes," Jake answered.

"Why?" I asked.

"She wanted YouBite to stay as it is," Jake said.

"Because if it became public, she thought you would sell it off like you did with your last company, and she would end up without a job and waiting for you to start another one after how long," I said.

"She did say that," Jake said. "I talked to her over the phone, and she said some pretty derogatory things about you, about me, and well…she was just so bitter. She thought she should have been made a partner at the last company, and this one."

"She told me you and her were together in a relationship," I said.

"I must admit we did casually hook up early on in college and throughout, but we were never boyfriend and girlfriend. We just didn't click in that way," Jake said.

"Oh," I looked down.

Jake tilted my head up so he was eye-to-eye with me. "I never had a relationship with that woman. The only woman I ever felt like I wanted a relationship with is you."

"But you were so cold to me," I said.

"I'm sorry I came across like that to you," Jake said. "There's something I've been keeping close to my chest for a while. Only just a few of my close friends, my parents, and eventually Cindy knew. When I'm focused on work, I'm in a zone. No social life. No love life. Nothing. I forget the world around me. I can blame it on being on the Spectrum growing up, but I've also learned that I can open myself up to balancing both work and a personal life." Jake blushed then.

Blushed. Adorably.

So Jake had autism.

Was that why I couldn't read his mind?

"Something about you helped break through that wall. I kept getting thoughts, images, ideas about you when I should have been thinking about work. I couldn't help myself. I thought of you constantly."

"You did?" I asked.

"You seemed so familiar but also new," Jake said.

Hmmm.

Do you remember me, Jake? From the restaurant?

I was so tempted to ask him but said nothing.

"Okay," I finally said as I got up and grabbed my purse. "Let's go to the restaurant. I'm starved."

Jake clapped his hands, "Excellent, the food is top-notched."

I had to hide my smile. He had to know that restaurant was my father's. We signed Chen's Family Cuisine on as a partner for YouBite. Maybe he's forgotten? Maybe he's just pulling my leg? In either case, I played along. "

"But first, let me get changed. I know that restaurant well, and I have to look presentable first. Maybe you'll find your answer there?"

"Maybe," Jake said, looking at me mysteriously.

Chapter 16

<u>Charisma</u>

As we made our way to the restaurant, we chatted idly about the orders and the mix up and Harold's part in it all.

The moment we entered the crowded restaurant, Sally looked at us, her eyes wide with surprise and her lips just aching to say something.

As Jake headed to his usual table, she eyed me and made a series of silly gestures, all essentially saying "what are you doing with him here?"

"Jake wanted to come here for Christmas dinner. Seems like a tradition he's always kept."

"Does he remember you as the server who has waited on him all these years every Christmas?" Sally asked.

"I don't know," I said. "He didn't say anything about it. And he seemed to have forgotten that our restaurant had signed onto being a vendor/partner of YouBite's newest product line."

"Strange," Sally said. "Does he have selective memory?"

"Perhaps," I said. "I just found out he has Autism, but that shouldn't have affected his memory. Only that he is highly focused on certain details while not being focused on social details. At least that's what I think he's said about why he acted the way he did towards me."

"Oh, okay," Sally said.

I headed back to Jake.

"Looks like a busy night," I said as Jake sat down. "I'll be right back."

"Where are you going?"

I continued as if I hadn't heard him and went into the kitchen.

Dad was rushing about cooking three different dishes at the same time while Tammy was tending to another two pots.

"Need a hand, Dad?" I said.

"Does it show?" he said in his ever-comical way.

"I've never seen the place like this," I said. "What's going on?"

"Power outage," he said as he huffed and puffed, stirring a big heavy pot of rice. "Los Angeles is in the dark. Can you imagine? And on Christmas night. Those who didn't get their turkey in the oven early enough are out of luck… and…" He pointed his wooden spoon toward the dining room. "… they're all out there wanting a good homecooked meal."

"I'll be right back."

Chinatown Christmas
(Chen Family Cuisine #1)

Grabbing a notepad and a pen, I rushed out to the dining room and back to Jake. "The owners are really swamped," I said, ready to take his order. "What will you have?"

He looked at me with a quizzical gaze. His lips parted, then closed again. His eyes narrowed, then popped open again. He looked around, then back at me.

"You said that you know the owners here, right?"

"That's right."

"And, does that mean that you've worked here before?"

I nodded.

"And do you sometimes work here on Christmas day?"

Laughing, I nodded again. "Well, well, well," I said with a teasing lilt. "I thought you'd never remember."

"Oh, damn," he said as he brought his palm to his forehead. "I can't believe I forgot this is your family's restaurant. Chen Family Cuisine. This restaurant is also a partner of YouBite."

"Yes," I smiled. "It's about time you remembered."

Jake shook his head. "That explains so much."

"What do you mean?"

"The connection. You, this place. I mean, like why I've always liked coming here on Christmas day. There's something about this place... the atmosphere. I never fail to get a sense of hope, a sense of warmth when I'm here. It's as if my spirit is lifted. It's a real boost to my morale."

"And?"

"It was you all along, the woman who had always waited on me on Christmas Day."

With my pen ready, I looked at him. "It took you a while to realize this," I laughed. "And what do you have when you come here?"

"The Many Treasures Tea and Thousand Years Thousand Ways Tofu Dish."

"Hm," I murmured softly. "We only serve that dish on Christmas."

I looked at him, remembering the recipes that I'd seen in that ancient book. They held powerful magic.

"I'll be right back," I said, leaving him to return to the kitchen.

"Hey," he called out. "Wait a second."

"Yeah?"

He looked sheepishly at me as he stood up. "I'd like to…" He looked toward the kitchen. "I mean… can I…?"

I smiled, happy to see he wanted to meet my family. "Sure," I said as I reached out to take his hand. "Come on."

"Hey, everybody," I called out when we reached the kitchen. "I'd like you all to meet my boss, Mr. Austin."

He leaned closer to me. "I think it's about time you started calling me Jake."

I chuckled. "Dad," I called out to him as he continued to race from one pot to the other. "I want you to meet Jake."

With sweat on his brow and a tired grin on his face, he rushed over to Jake, quickly shook his hand and returned to his pots calling out over his shoulder, "Nice to meet you."

"And this is Sally," I went on. "You two briefly met at the entrance to YouBite."

"Sorry if I came off as a little rude," he said.

I thought she was going to say something smart, but she simply smiled and said, "Hello."

"And Tammy, the marketing genius," I went on, gesturing toward her.

"You saved the day," Jake said as he vigorously shook her hand.

"And, of course, the name that will be on your new product this year..." I gestured for my mom to come to us. "This is the woman herself... Dazzle."

"It's a pleasure," Jake said.

"Okay," I said as I nudged Jake to the kitchen door. "We'll let them get back to work."

Jake pulled his hand free of my grasp and shrugged his jacket off. After hanging it on a hook by the door, he rolled up his sleeves.

"What are you doing?" I said.

His response was to wash his hands and head to the cutting board. "You need carrots? Onions? Celery? Chopped? Minced? Sliced?"

"Jake?"

"Hey," he said with a smile. "After everything that you all have done for me, chopping up a few vegetables is the least that I can do."

"But..."

"Don't sweat it, Charisma," he said. "I love to cook. Why do you think I started a company like YouBite?" He laughed. "Besides, you guys are swamped. Did you see that line outside?"

Smiling, I, too, went to the kitchen counter to help out. While Jake went through an entire basket of vegetables, I helped where I could, stirring pots, searing beef, boiling broccoli… and going out to serve the ever-growing crowd… whatever it took.

"You're good at this," Dad said as he checked in on Jake.

"Can he come help us out every night?" Sally joked.

"Another couple just walked in," Tammy called out. "Can someone go see to them?"

"I'll go," I said, smiling at the comradery that was already apparent between my dad and Jake.

I headed out to the overcrowded dining room and went to the older couple standing at the door. "Hi," I said. "Merry Christmas. We presently have a twenty-minute wait for a table."

"That's fine," the old man said. "We'll wait."

"That's right," the woman said. "I don't mind the wait."

I pulled out my notepad. "Your name, please."

"Austin," the man said. "William Austin."

I looked at them and was about to ask but held my tongue.

Austin? The same Austin? Could it be?

I returned to the kitchen and went to Jake who'd taken on the task of cutting cooked chicken into tiny cubes.

"Jake?"

"Yep."

"Would you happen to know a William Austin?"

He stopped cutting the chicken and looked at me. "William? Really?"

"Yeah," I said. "They're out there waiting for a table."

He went to the door and peeked into the dining room. "Oh, my God."

"Are those your parents?" I said.

He nodded and looked at me with a boyish grin.

Ten minutes later, a table cleared, and Jake's parents were seated. I took their order and when it was ready, Jake grabbed the tray.

"I'll take this," he said as he headed out.

We all stood in the kitchen door, looking on as Jake went out to surprise his parents.

"Isn't that sweet," Mom said as Jake hugged his parents.

Jake gestured for me to come out to meet his parents. I walked over to their table and greeted them with a welcoming smile. "Very nice to meet you, Mr. and Mrs. Austin," I said. "Of course everything you order will be on the house."

"Oh, isn't that sweet?" Mrs. Austin said. "So you're Charisma, the girl Jake told me about."

I glanced over at Jake who looked suddenly shy.

When we realized that you wouldn't make it home, we decided to visit instead, and when we saw the way you looked at Charisma, we understood the real reason you chose to stay in town for Christmas. Our baby has found his girl.

I was suddenly embarrassed to realize that I'd just read his mother's mind.

We approve. She seems like such a nice girl and so polished.

It was so easy… so clear. Even his father was easy to read.

Then why was it so hard to read Jake. While I'd come to read him slightly, it was difficult.

I smiled as I looked at him. Then again, like a chip of ice that been hammered off, he was getting easier and easier to read.

Jake smiled, his eyes filled with happiness. "I can't believe I have all the people I love and care for right here tonight with me."

He kissed the top of my head and pulled me closer to him.

Yeah, Charisma, I don't know when it happened, but you're someone I don't want to spend Christmas without.

Epilogue

There.

I couldn't believe I was able to finally read Jake Austin's mind.

What happened?

The next morning, the day after Christmas, as exhausted as I was, I made it to the office early, eager to see how things had turned out following Cindy and Harold's sabotage of the launch.

As I came to Jake's office, his doors were wide open. Already seated at his desk, his eyes were on the screen in front of him, a large cup of coffee in his hand.

"Dare I ask?" I whispered, afraid of the results of the launch.

He turned to me, an adorable grin on his face. "Ask away, Charisma."

"How'd it go?"

"Perfect. Better than expected. We did it, Charisma. We did it." He stood and came around his desk, grasping my shoulders. "And it's all thanks to you. You did it. You made this launch a success, despite Cindy and Harold's fail attempt to ruin everything."

"How did we do?" I said, eager to know more. "What are the numbers?"

He released me and returned to his desk, turning his screen to me. "Yesterday; 125,000."

I was speechless.

"We sold 125,000 gift cards. 125,000 subscriptions to our yearly dining program."

Chinatown Christmas
(Chen Family Cuisine #1)

I stared at the screen, unable to believe the numbers. I'd hoped for a thousand… maybe a few thousand. But this…

He put his hand to my shoulder. "This is all on you, Char. You're the one who thought up this brilliant plan… and it worked. Damn, I think it worked better than the way I'd originally planned."

I leaned into him, suddenly weak with fatigue, with relief, with happiness. He pulled me into his arms and held me tight.

"Everything about you is better than I'd originally planned," he whispered as he cupped my cheeks. He leaned in, pressing his warm lips over mine.

I got lost in the embrace, in the heat of the searing kiss that I never wanted to end. But he pulled back, breathless as he looked into my eyes.

"I noticed you from the start," he said.

"When you hired me?"

"No. Before that. The very first time I went to your family's restaurant. My first Christmas there. I saw you and was mesmerized. You were so beautiful. So elegant and graceful. You wore a beautiful dress covered with golden sequins. You were a vision, a goddess… an empress."

My cheeks were suddenly aflame as I listened to him. He'd seen me. He'd noticed me. "You never said anything to me."

"I was too nervous," he said. "How could I make a move on you? I didn't feel worthy. And then, on top of it, I tried the food, and I was blown away. It was like I'd been hit with some magical spell or something. After that, I knew I'd have to come back every Christmas."

"Well, I'm certainly glad that you did, Jake Austin," I said. "Every Christmas after that first time that you came, I looked forward to seeing you again. There was something comforting in seeing you at your regular table. Then fate brought me to work for you."

He pulled me in and kissed me. "I believe in fate, Charisma," he whispered. "Charisma. I just love how your name reminds me of Christmas, only you're here with me all year long."

I smiled. "Does that mean that I'm no longer just a temporary replacement for Janet?"

"After the miracle that you performed, I'm never letting you go."

Leaning into him, I laughed.

"Actually," he said. "I received an email from Janet this morning."

"Oh?"

"She's decided to stay home with her baby," he said. "She won't be coming back. So… that means that the job is yours, permanently… if you'll have it."

"Ha! Yes!" I let out with excitement. "Of course I want it."

He hugged me, so hard that he nearly squeezed the breath out of me. "And you won't have to worry about Harold," he said. "Not only is he never coming back, but you can handpick your research team as you see fit."

I pulled back and looked into his eyes. He was a far cry from the grump I'd first met. "I'm glad you're not ever going to spend Christmas sitting at a table in a restaurant all alone again."

"I'm never intending on spending Christmas without you," he whispered. "Not if I can help it. Because you, Charisma Chen, are not going anywhere without me from now on. I love you."

I looked into Jake's eyes, and saw the clouds have disappeared around them. The stress that had blocked him from me was gone.

It didn't take a psychic to read what he had in mind, but I wanted him to know what I had in mind, too.

"I love you too, Jake, grump and all," I said, kissing him softly on his lips. "And if I didn't say it yesterday, I wish you a very very merry, happy, and prosperous Christmas and New Year's."

"It already is," Jake said, kissing me back. "It already is."

****

Enjoyed Chinatown Christmas? Please consider letting others know posting a review on your favorite book retail site.

Want more books like Chinatown Christmas from Kailin Gow?

Check out:

RAMEN ROMANCE:
An Enemies to Lover Romantic Comedy

https://www.amazon.com/gp/product/B09WL7FLF4

They're bringing the heat....

She's the heiress to a ramen noodle food company and he's the gorgeous but arrogant gourmet chef who sees everything her family's processed foods company produces as evil and vile.

Winona "Winnie" Wu has never lost a battle before, and when Peter Jacobs openly protests the noodle company in a contest, Winnie can't help but go head-to-head against this arrogant know-it-all.

What could this cover model-turned chef know about real ramen?

What could a silver-spooned heiress know about serving real food?

In this romantic comedy/drama with two hot-headed rivals, food, fists, and more would be thrown until they realize there might be a reason more personal to their heated exchanges than just food....

**Ramen Romance is an Enemies to Lover Romance with slow burn passion.

Bubble Tea Book Club: A Women's Fiction Thriller

https://www.amazon.com/dp/B09XN2F6DT

At the Bubble Tea Book Club, members discuss books, movies, men while having their favorite bubble tea and snacks, but when a terrible tragedy happens to one of them, they turn their amateur-sleuthing minds to help solve the mystery.

Sweetest Season: An Age Gap Sweet Romance

https://www.amazon.com/dp/B09XMYDM32

With all the swoons and heartfelt of a k-drama...

Kandi Lin is the cute but quirky owner of a sauce and seasoning company in a Coastal California town, who spends all her time watching dramas when she is not coming up with a new flavor or running her company.

He is an aimless young blonde too-hot-for-his-own-good surfer who happens to be what the temp agency sent over when she fell ill. Facing a shortage of good reliable staff choices, she had to settle for this temp with an arrogant attitude. Not being able to shake off the illness, which causes her to lose her sense of taste and smell, as much as she couldn't stand the guy, her sudden condition causes her to rely on the new hotshot assistant she just hired more than she expected.

Chinatown Christmas
(Chen Family Cuisine #1)

Even at her home. Everything about him was so wrong.

But then everything about her, to him, felt so right.

Forbidden never felt so sweet.

**Sweetest Season is an enemy-to-lover sweet romance but with a bit of slow burn. Appropriate for TV-14 readers.

About the Author Kailin Gow

Kailin Gow once played keyboards and drums for a girl band that she formed during college at the University of California at Irvine. She was also the singer and songwriter for her band. During junior high, she played the violin, chairing her school's orchestra. Today, she not only writes books, but screenplays, directs and film award-winning films, and composes original music for the films.

From visiting Romania, ALA YALSA Award-winning and Million-Selling Author Kailin Gow was asked to write stories about vampires; visiting the Black Forest in Germany and seeing the castles of Europe inspired her to write fantasy; visiting Asia's mystical mountains inspired her to write action adventure and mythological dystopians.

Chinatown Christmas
(Chen Family Cuisine #1)

From her experience in college as a peer counselor and her volunteer work with women's shelters, she was inspired to write contemporary romance with social issues for women, new adults, young adults, and teens. Having faced adversity, including battling stereotypes and bullying, Kailin Gow has become a well-known speaker and influential figure in media. Her adventurous bold spirit has taken her around the world, where she has ridden on top of elephants through jungles, hand-fed sting rays, studied kung fu from a Shaolin Temple monk, and learned cooking from a celebrity chef. She is a USA Today Bestselling author and has been a #1 Amazon bestselling author over two-hundred times. Her Bitter Frost Series is in development as a TV Series, and her contemporary romance Loving Summer is set to become a feature film. An multi-award-winning filmmaker, director, and actress; Kailin's films have premiered at Cannes, Los Angeles,

Rome, England, Paris, Korea, Japan, and even in India's Ministry of Culture.

Compelled to write her first fiction book because of 9/11, Kailin Gow now has over 680 books published under Kailin Gow and various Pen Names in many genres. As a speaker and host, she has hosted international shows at the Pasadena Civic Auditorium, been a celebrity judge at beauty pageants, been a judge for writing contests, and hosted television series. She was featured as an Indie Author Success Story on the homepage of Amazon.com for a month and is also included in Amazon's book called Transformations. She is the first Asian American to have been featured on Amazon's homepage as an Author Success Story, and the first to have sold over a million books.

Chinatown Christmas
(Chen Family Cuisine #1)

Get a Free Romance and notices of new releases from Kailin here:

https://dl.bookfunnel.com/qgu4l0rizc

Bookbub
https://www.bookbub.com/authors/kailin-gow

Amazon Author Page
https://www.amazon.com/Kailin-
Gow/e/B002BMAEH4